The Preacher's
Addiction

A novel by

R.T. Haymon

Acknowledgments

Thanks to all the people associated with RTH publishing that assisted in the publishing of this book: Robert L. Miles, L.J. Simmons and Angalene Harris.

1. **Woe** be unto the pastors that destroy and scatter the sheep of my pasture! saith the Lord

2. Therefore thus saith the Lord God of Israel against the pastors that feed my people; Ye have scattered my flock, and driven them away, and have not visited them: behold, I will visit upon you the evil of your doings, saith the Lord.

Jeremiah 23:1-2

King James Version

Table of Contents

Prologue

*"Don't ever stop praying, and always remember that
God loves you. He has already forgiven you, so forgive
yourself... and no matter what, I'm here for you."*

-Reverend Stokes

The flight from Atlanta to Spokane was so peaceful and serene that Kevin wished it would never end. He sat in his window seat and fantasized like a child. He imagined he could freeze time and remain on the flight forever, soaring in the clouds, trapped within his own reality. He was eager to escape his past, a past marked by ridicule and shame. But also, he was nervous and unsure about his future. He looked over at Reverend Stokes asleep in the seat beside him. He smiled at the old man. With his head laid back, and his mouth wide open, he snored peacefully.

Reverend Stokes was his father in the ministry, his spiritual teacher, and most importantly his friend. He had sat under his tutelage for more than twenty years, learning and growing, while at the same time, enjoying the blessings that trickled down from the Reverend s mantle into his own life.

Now that he had lost his wife, his two kids, *and* his self-respect, Reverend Stokes was all he had left. He had been Kevin's rock from the beginning and now he was holding his hand and supporting his rehabilitation.

Kevin sat motionless as the plane landed. Sweat moistened his palms, and his legs trembled as his fellow passengers exited the plane.

Reverend Stokes noticed Kevin's quivering. He gave him a firm pat on the knee as he stood. "Come on Son, it's time to go."

The sound of Reverend Stokes' voice gave Kevin a boost of courage and reassured him that God was still on his side.

The Uber driver drove them from the airport to the suburbs of Spokane. The drive gave Kevin one last opportunity to thank his mentor for his support. As they drove up to the massive compound, Kevin read the large blue and white sign at the entrance. *Welcome to the Josephine Clark Addiction Center.* His heart fluttered and sweat gathered in his armpits. He wanted to turn back around and say forget it, and if his Pastor had not been by his side, he would have.

"We're here," the Uber driver announced as he parked the car in front of the admissions building. The driver popped the trunk, and Kevin grabbed a small suitcase. According to the online brochure, he could only pack one piece of luggage, and cellphones were prohibited.

"Hi, Mr. Tyler. Welcome to the Josephine Clark Addiction Center," a bubbly, middle-aged woman greeted him at the reception desk. "Is this your father?" she asked.

"No, Ma'am. He's my Pastor," Kevin corrected her with a proud smile as he put his arm around Reverend Stokes' shoulders.

"According to our policy, you have thirty minutes to say goodbye to your loved ones and then he will have to leave," she said politely.

"I don't need thirty minutes. The car is still waiting for me, so I'll only take a couple," Reverend Stokes said. He turned and faced Kevin. He put both of his hands on Kevin's shoulders, closed his eyes then lowered his head.

Kevin knew the position. He closed his eyes, lowered his head, and took a deep breath as his spiritual Father prayed for him. After a few minutes, Reverend Stokes gave him a firm hug and whispered a few words of encouragement in his ear.

"Don't ever stop praying, and always remember that God loves you. He has already forgiven you, so forgive yourself... and no matter what, I'm here for you." He gave Kevin a pat on the back, turned, and walked out the door.

Kevin sighed as he watched his mentor get into the car and ride off. A feeling reminiscent of his first day of preschool assailed him. He remembered how scared and alone he felt when his mother left him in that strange room with all those unfamiliar faces.

The next day, Kevin sat in a circle of fold-out chairs. He looked around at the different faces sitting in the circle with him. There were about twenty-five in all, male and female from all levels of society, all dealing with their addictions.

"We have a new member in our group. Please stand and introduce yourself?" the group therapist said to Kevin.

He eased up out his chair with his head hung low and shoulders slumped. "My name is Kevin Tyler," he mumbled.

"Hi, Kevin, welcome to our group," everyone responded in unison.

"Since this is your first day here, will you please share your story with us?" the therapist asked.

Kevin nodded and began to speak. "Like I've already said, my name is Kevin Tyler and I'm here, so it's obvious that I'm an addict, but my addiction is not to drugs or alcohol, or any other type of substance. I'm addicted to sex... I'm a sex addict!" Kevin paused to catch his breath. That was his first time saying those words out loud. Tears trickled down his face. He tried not to cry, but those words made him realize how much he had lost and how far he had fallen.

"It's alright, Kevin," the group therapist tried to encourage him.

After regaining his composure, Kevin continued. "Until recently, I didn't know sexual addiction was real. I went from being a thug to a preacher and eventually a sex addict. My story began twenty years ago..."

****

Chapter 1

"No risk, no reward. We gotta get this money."

-Kevin Tyler

Atlanta, Georgia 2003

"**D**amn, Big Mike. This is the worst drought I've ever seen. We only have one key left and it's gonna be gone by tonight," Kevin complained as he darted his brand-new Mercedes through the busy Atlanta traffic.

Big Mike and Kevin were cousins, sons of twin sisters. Their mothers were pregnant with them at the same time, but Kevin was a week older. They grew up pretending to be brothers and began selling crack cocaine on the street corners when they were just twelve years old. Now, at twenty-one, their drug operation spanned from Atlanta to Fort Valley, Georgia, and up to Chattanooga, Tennessee.

Kevin was the brains of the business and while at six-foot-six and three hundred pounds, Big Mike was the muscle. Kevin took pride in being a low-key drug dealer. A quiet millionaire is how he described himself, and despite his age, he was already an up-and-coming player in Atlanta's booming real estate market.

"I talked to Jake in Houston, and he won't have any product until next month," Big Mike said.

"What about Carlos and Pedro?"

"It's tight in Jacksonville too. We can get it, but at double the normal price." Big Mike shrugged his shoulders.

"Damn!" Kevin slammed his fist against the steering wheel. "We need to cop at least twenty bricks and I ain't paying double for that much yay... get in touch with Cortez and tell him we're coming to Miami."

"You know those Cubans down in Miami are cut-throat during drought seasons. Are you sure you wanna take that risk?" Big Mike cautioned.

"No risk, no reward. We gotta get this money. If we can re-up in Miami, we're gonna make a killing during this drought, so be ready to leave for Florida in the morning."

Big Mike nodded his head and made the phone call.

Once the deal was sealed, Kevin dropped Big Mike off and headed to his parents' house in College Park.

**

"What's up, Momma?" Kevin asked as he stepped inside the house. "I smell barbecue, what are y'all cooking?"

"Your father is in the backyard grilling pork chops and ribs," his mother replied as she kissed him on the cheek.

"Why would Pops invite me over for dinner then turn around and cook pork chops? He knows I ain't gonna eat no swine."

"He knew you were coming over. He has the fish fryer out there just for you...he has something to talk to you about."

"Okay, Momma," Kevin said and made his way to the backyard.

"What's up, Pops? Momma said you had something important you wanted to discuss, and since you pulled out the fish fryer, I'm assuming it must be serious. You know fish is my weakness." Kevin smiled as he picked up a piece of fish and began eating.

"Yeah, have a seat, son." He motioned for Kevin to sit down. "You know your mother and I have been going to a different church for over a year now. The Pastor's name is Reverend Stokes. He's a good man and he's really bringing the Word of God."

"Okay, but what that got to do with me?"

"I know what you do for a living. You're a grown man and I don't fuss at you about your business, but as your father, I want you to do me one favor."

"What is it?" Kevin asked suspiciously.

"God has put it on my heart to ask you to come to church tomorrow with your mother and me."

"Is that all you had to talk to me about?" Kevin sounded relieved.

"Yes." His father nodded.

"Pops, you don't have to bribe me with a fish dinner to get me to go to church with you. I'll go," Kevin said, and they shared a hug. Kevin didn't want to go, but he thought that since his father had enough courage to ask him, the least he could do was say yes and show up.

****

Chapter 2

"The only difference is that sanctified girls pull their skirts up while hood girls pull their pants down"

-Big Mike

Kevin and Big Mike pulled into the church parking lot about ten minutes before the morning service began.

"Man, why I gotta go in there with you? Uncle Robert asked you to go to church, not me," Big Mike complained to Kevin.

"Because as soon as we leave here, we're heading straight for Florida." Kevin frowned. "Now give me your Rolex and your necklace...and take those earrings out."

"Why?"

"Because this ain't no night club. We don't wanna go in there looking like no drug dealers. I've warned you about being too flashy anyway. We're trying to blend in, not stand out."

"Come on, Kev. You're killing my swag. I might meet one of those fine sanctified girls with the big booty and the tight skirt. They say those sanctified girls got that bomb between their legs." Big Mike laughed as he took his jewelry off and handed it to Kevin, who quickly hid the items inside a secret compartment he had installed behind one of his air vents.

"What's the *only* difference between having sex with a sanctified girl and a hood girl?" Big Mike asked with a silly grin on his face.

"I don't know." Kevin laughed.

"The only difference is that sanctified girls pull their skirts up, while hood girls pull their pants down," Big Mike said, and burst out into a loud cackle. Kevin couldn't help but laugh along with him as they got out of the car.

They entered the church and quietly sat on the last pew in the very back. Even without their jewelry, the two stood out like sore thumbs. They had that street hustler's glow, a look that said young, rich, and dangerous.

Kevin's eyes scanned the church. He noticed there were plenty of good-looking women stirring around.

"You're right," he whispered to Big Mike.

"Right about what?"

"There *are* a lot of fine women up in here."

"I told you." Big Mike smiled.

While they checked out the women, Kevin noticed his father looking at him. They made eye contact, and he acknowledged Kevin's presence with a nod and a proud fatherly smile.

Impressed by the choir, Kevin found himself moving his head and tapping his feet to the music. He was enjoying the service. Except for his grandmother's funeral, it had been over eight years since he had been inside of a church.

After the choir had finished, Reverend Stokes stood to deliver his sermon. He was a tall, dark-skinned man with a bald head and white facial hair. And when he opened his mouth to speak, his voice sounded like the actor James Earl Jones. Kevin and Big Mike paid attention as he preached a message about the power of God's forgiveness.

At the end of his sermon, Reverend Stokes stood in the pulpit and made an altar call. "Is there anyone here today that wants to be saved? If you would like to accept Jesus Christ as your personal Lord and Savior, please come to the altar now," he said as the choir sang softly.

Big Mike nudged Kevin with his elbow, "C'mon cuz, let's go get saved."

"Quit playin' around," Kevin whispered back.

"I ain't playin.' I need Jesus in my life," Big Mike said and then he stood and walked toward the altar.

"Wait... don't be playin' with God," Kevin whispered as he tried to grab his cousin's wrist. Big Mike turned and gave him a look like he was dead serious and then he turned back around and walked to the altar.

Kevin looked on with amazement as his cousin stood at the altar and accepted Christ in his life. He could not believe his eyes. Big Mike cried like a baby as Reverend Stokes prayed with him. The choir continued to sing softly, and Reverend Stokes prayed with all the people that came to the altar to receive Christ in their life.

After the altar call, Big Mike returned to his seat with tears in his eyes. Kevin could see that he was sincere, so he decided not to say anything to him while they were still inside the church.

I'm gonna cuss him out as soon as we get out to the car, Kevin thought as he tried to ignore Big Mike sitting next to him sniffling and crying. But Kevin's thoughts were suddenly interrupted by the sound of Reverend Stokes' voice. He stood in front of the podium with his microphone in one hand and pointing in Kevin's direction with his other hand.

"You, young man. Come up here. The Lord has given me a Word for you," he said as all the eyes in the church turned and looked in Kevin's direction.

He glanced around, pointed at himself, and mouthed, "Who me?"

"Yes, you, son," the man of God said. "Come up here." He motioned for him to get up.

Kevin reluctantly stood and walked to where the pastor was standing. Reverend Stokes stood in front of Kevin, placed one hand on his shoulder, and began speaking to him.

"The Lord has given me a word for you." The Reverend's voice boomed through the giant floor speakers.

Kevin nodded his head. He wasn't feeling this religious display, nor did he appreciate the Reverend calling him out in front of all those people.

"What's your name, Son?"

"Kevin Tyler."

"Well, Kevin Tyler, I don't know anything about you. Until right now, I didn't even know your name, but God told me to tell you that whatever you plan to do when you leave here today is going to fail. God wants you to know that only death and destruction will come from it.

Kevin stood there with a blank expression on his face. He was trying not to show any emotion. *I gotta keep my poker face. I can't let him play me with this slick preacher talk.*

"Do you hear me, son?" Reverend Stokes asked, snapping Kevin out of his thoughts.

"Yes, sir," Kevin nodded and then he rudely turned around and walked back to his seat.

As soon as the church service was over, Kevin grabbed Big Mike by his arm and pulled him outside.

"C'mon let's go," he said as he rushed Big Mike to the car.

When they got in the car, Kevin snapped on him and began shouting. "What the hell is wrong with you? Why did you go up there?"

"I don't know, I just felt something," Big Mike said softly as he shrugged his shoulders.

"You didn't feel nuthin'! You let that preacher and that soft music trick you into gettin' saved," Kevin shot back at him.

"Naw, Kev, it wasn't like that. I felt like God was speaking to me."

"Yeah, whatever. Let's just hit the road and get this yay."

"Didn't you hear what the Reverend said to you?" Big Mike cautioned.

"Yeah, I heard that garbage he was talking, but I gotta gc make this money. I can't be worried about some religious old man trying to jinx my operation," Kevin snarled.

****

Chapter 3

"I got saved this morning. I'm going to heaven."

-Big Mike

Big Mike barely said a word to Kevin during the long drive to Miami. He just listened to the radio and stared out the window. For hours, they rode without saying a word to each other. It was an awkward ride, and Kevin could sense Big Mike had a lot on his mind. He loved his cousin like a brother. They grew up doing everything together. They joined the basketball and football teams together. And even though soccer was Kevin's least favorite sport, he joined the team to support Big Mike.

Kevin smiled in his head as he thought about the day he lost his virginity to Daphanie Bird. Big Mike had hidden under the bed, tickling his feet. He didn't want to lose him to the "church life." His cousin was the only person he trusted in the drug game. *I can't do this by myself,* he thought as he sped his Mercedes down I-75.

Big Mike read the sign as they turned off on the exit. *"Welcome to Miami, Florida."* They stopped for gas and headed to a hotel.

As they pulled into the hotel parking lot, Big Mike turned to Kevin. "This is my last trip. When we get back to Atlanta, I'm shuttin' it down. I'm done selling drugs."

"You're just talking. Wait 'til we get back home and you see all that money rollin' in," Kevin said with a dismissive tone. But when Big Mike didn't respond, he smashed on the brakes and threw the car in park. "Just get the money out of the trunk. I'm gonna go in and get our room," Kevin snapped. He opened the glove compartment and pulled out two pistols. "Here, take this." He shoved one of the guns into Big Mike's hand, and then he got out of the car and slammed the door.

Big Mike shook his head. He could see Kevin was upset. But he knew Kevin loved him, and because of that love, he would eventually come around and support his decision.

The money for their drug deal was in a duffle bag, stashed inside a hidden compartment in the trunk. Big Mike had to use a socket wrench to open the hidden compartment. It took him about ten minutes to remove the false bottom to get to the three-hundred thousand dollars in cash.

**

Marlo and Peewee pulled into the hotel parking lot and waited. Kevin and Big Mike were so distracted during their drive that they didn't realize they were being followed. Peewee and Marlo had been tailing them since before they went to church that morning. As soon as Big Mike made the deal with Cortez to buy the twenty kilos of cocaine, Cortez called two of his goons he had already dispatched to Atlanta to stick up any drug dealer moving large quantities of cocaine. Drought season brought the worst out of the drug game. Even the major drug dealers began setting up other dealers to keep their cash flow going. During drought season, most dealers either went broke, started robbing, or got robbed.

"Just be patient," Marlo said to Peewee. "Cortez promised this lick would be worth at least three hundred G's."

Peewee flashed his platinum grin and nodded his head as he clutched his pistol. The two goons had been talking from Atlanta to Miami about how they would spend their cut of the money.

"Look, he's going in the trunk," Peewee said, tapping Marlo on the arm.

"Get ready. As soon as we see the money, we're gonna make our move," Marlo instructed.

After about ten minutes, Big Mike pulled a duffle bag out of the trunk and began resealing the hidden compartment.

"I see a duffle bag. C'mon let's go," Marlo ordered.

They quickly snuck up on Big Mike while his back was turned and pointed their guns at him.

"Give me the bag," Peewee growled.

Big Mike didn't hesitate. He immediately handed the bag over and put his hands in the air. Any other time, he would have been trying to figure out a way to make a move on the two robbers. He could have easily dipped behind the car, pulled his gun from the small of his back, and turn the situation into a shootout, but he was relieved. He didn't want to do the drug deal anyway.

Now Kevin will see that God was really speaking through Reverend Stokes, he thought as he stood with his hands raised.

Kevin walked out of the hotel just as the two goons were getting away with the bag of money.

"Aww, shit." Kevin stopped in his tracks. "They just jacked Big Mike." He quickly pulled his gun from the small of his back and began shooting at the two robbers.

Kevin's shots seemed to come out of nowhere as Peewee and Marlo tried to get away with the money. They instinctively returned fire as they tried to scramble to their car. But Kevin was relentless in his pursuit, he moved with determination as he focused on the duffle bag in Peewee's hand. As soon as Peewee made it to the car, two bullets ripped through his back. He screamed in pain as he opened the passenger door. He dropped the bag and collapsed halfway into the car. Marlo quickly pulled him in the car as he tried to reach over Peewee's limp body to grab the bag of money. But Kevin was still shooting and closing in fast, so Marlo retreated and left the money while speeding out of the hotel parking lot.

Kevin grabbed the bag of money and walked back toward his car. He suddenly realized he didn't see Big Mike. He dropped the duffle bag and sprinted to the car. The horrific sight caused his knees to buckle. Big Mike was lying on the ground in a pool of blood.

"MIKE!" Kevin shouted as he kneeled. "Come on, cuz, don't die on me," Kevin cried as he held Big Mike in his arms. "SOMEBODY HELP! PLEASE, SOMEBODY! CALL 9-1-1," he screamed as he nervously scanned the parking lot for assistance.

"Don't cry, Kev," Big Mike struggled to talk. He was wheezing and coughing blood. He grabbed Kevin's shirt, looked into his eyes, and with his last breaths, he pushed his words out in a painful whisper. "I got saved this morning...I'm going to heaven." He released Kevin's shirt and died in his arms.

Kevin screamed at the top of his lungs while cradling Big Mike's lifeless body.

****

Chapter 4

"I'll tell you what, son. Try God's way for thirty days, and if you don't like it, you can always go back to hustling and running the streets...

-Reverend Stokes

Tears streamed down Kevin's face as he stared at Big Mike's lifeless body. He looked so peaceful as he lay in the plush white and gold casket. He looked as if he were asleep. Kevin cracked a soft smile through his tears. He wished he could just reach down, shake Big Mike, and then wait for him to wake up. But he knew this would be his last time seeing his favorite cousin.

He carefully leaned over into the casket, kissed Big Mike's forehead, and whispered to him, "I love you cuz. I'm sorry I didn't listen to you. I don't know what I'm going to do without you."

But no matter how hard Kevin tried, he couldn't find the strength to walk away from the casket. He wanted to stand there and talk to Big Mike's body until he miraculously came back to life.

After about ten minutes of leaning over into the casket, Kevin felt a hand touch his shoulder.

It was his mother. "C'mon, Kevin, let him go," she said softly to him.

Kevin looked at her, and then he looked around the church. It took him a moment to realize he was at a funeral. He had been in a trance. His mind lost in his conversation with his dead cousin.

"Hold on, Momma, let me finish talking to Big Mike," he muttered back to her.

"That's enough, baby. He's gone. You've got to let him go." She gently tried to pull him away from the casket.

"STOP!" Kevin shouted as he jerked away from her. The air in the church went silent as all eyes locked on Kevin. "I'm not done," he continued to shout. "Look at him, he's not gone. He can still hear me," he yelled, and then burst into tears and sobbed loudly. "He can hear me, Momma...he can hear me."

Kevin turned back to Big Mike's casket and shouted hysterically at him. "You can hear me, cuz. Wake up. Quit playin' around and wake up."

Kevin's father and two of his uncles wrestled him away from Big Mike's casket. Kevin put up a passionate struggle until he finally collapsed in his father's arms. Reverend Stokes at once motioned for the men to bring Kevin into his office. They carried him out of the sanctuary and laid him down on the soft leather sofa in the Pastor's office.

"You all can leave, I'll keep an eye on him until he wakes up," Reverend Stokes promised.

"Are you sure?" Kevin's father asked.

"Yes, go ahead to the cemetery with your family. Your son will be fine right here. I won't take my eyes off him."

"Thank you, Pastor."

Reverend Stokes pulled a blanket out of his wardrobe closet and covered Kevin up to his chin. He turned on some gospel music, grabbed his Bible, and sat down in the leather office chair behind his desk.

Kevin awoke about an hour later, feeling groggy and sluggish, as if he had been out drinking the night before.

"How are you feeling?" Reverend Stokes asked in his deep, proper annunciating, James Earl Jones voice.

"Not good," Kevin said as he looked around the room. "Where am I?"

"You're in my office."

"How did I get in here?"

"You passed out, your father and your uncles carried you in here."

"Big Mike!" Kevin shouted and jumped up off the sofa. He opened the office door and noticed the empty pews. "Where is everybody? Where is Big Mike?"

"Calm down, son. Your father just called and said they are on their way back from the cemetery."

"From the cemetery!" Kevin repeated in a loud panicky voice. "How long was I out?"

"About an hour."

"You mean I missed his burial," Kevin cried. He dropped back down on the sofa, lowered his head, and wept. "I was supposed to help carry his casket."

Reverend Stokes leaned back in his chair and did not say a word. He understood that Kevin needed a moment to mourn. He had attended enough funerals to know that sometimes people just need to cry and release their grief.

Minutes had passed and Kevin continued to cry like a baby.

"Do you believe in heaven?" Reverend Stokes asked.

"Huh?" Kevin raised his head.

"I asked you if you believed in heaven."

"Yeah, of course, I believe in heaven." Kevin nodded with a curious expression on his face. He didn't understand why the pastor asked him that question.

"Your cousin is in heaven."

"Yeah-yeah, I know he's gone." Kevin rolled his eyes. "You don't have to pacify me with religion."

"I'm not trying to pacify you. I'm telling you the truth. Your cousin is not just gone. He's in heaven with Jesus. Your cousin died a saved man."

Kevin cracked a smile through his tears. "Do you really believe he's in heaven? He was only saved for a few hours."

"It doesn't matter whether you have been saved for five minutes or fifty years, if you repent of your sins and accept Jesus Christ as your personal Lord and Savior, you get to go to heaven. Jesus said in Mathew 19:30, '... *the first shall be last and the last shall be first.*'"

Kevin nodded his head, his eyes gleamed and his smile widened at the thought of Big Mike resting in heaven. "I can picture him up there chilling."

"You can't bring him back, but God can arrange it so that you can see him again," Reverend Stokes hinted.

Kevin's smile disappeared, quickly turning into a frown. "Don't do that." He stood and pointed his finger in the Reverend's face. "Don't sit there and try to trick me into accepting no Jesus."

"No one can trick you into accepting Christ. Either you answer his call, or you don't... And God is calling you, son...He wants you."

"What does He want with me?" Kevin's voice quivered. Reverend Stokes' words sent goosebumps all over his body.

"He wants to save your soul. He has a purpose for your life."

"Well, why did He kill Big Mike? What was His purpose for doing that?" Kevin slammed his fist on the sofa as he sat back down.

"God didn't kill Big Mike." Reverend Stokes shook his head in displeasure at Kevin's accusation against his Heavenly Father. "God saved his soul and now Big Mike is in heaven." He paused for a moment to look into Kevin's eyes. "Big Mike has served his purpose."

"And what was his purpose?" Kevin snapped.

"Big Mike's purpose was to bring *you* to Christ."

"He didn't have to die for that," Kevin sobbed and then lowered his head.

"Big Mike is in heaven, and he'll be waiting for you when you get there, if you make the right choice."

"I don't know, Rev. I'm a hustler, and this church life ain't for me."

"Just try God out. What do you have to lose?" Reverend Stokes said.

"I don't know." Kevin shrugged his shoulders.

"I'll tell you what, son. Try God's way for thirty days, and if you don't like it, you can always go back to hustling and running the streets. But you will never know whether it's for you or not if you don't try Him. You may never get this chance again. Tomorrow is not promised to any of us."

Now, tears trickled from the corner of the Reverend's eyes. He felt a heaviness in his heart for the young man sitting across from him.

Kevin looked into Reverend Stokes' eyes. He noticed the old man's tears and heard the sincerity in his voice. "Okay, I'll try God," he said, capitulating.

****

Chapter 5

"It takes courage to trust God to take us beyond what we know we can do."

-Reverend Stokes

Atlanta, GA 2023

It had been twenty years since Kevin first accepted Christ into his life, and he had never looked back, nor did he regret that fateful day in Reverend Stokes' office. He thanked God every day for saving his life, and at age forty-two, his life couldn't be any better. The real estate company he started before he accepted Christ in his life had grown over the years. He now owned property all over the state of Georgia as well as Texas, Alabama, and Tennessee.

God had also blessed him with a beautiful wife. He met René Thomas at church. A twenty-two-year-old virgin and recent graduate of Georgia State University. They had been married for seventeen years and had two wonderful kids, twelve-year-old Joann and ten-year-old Little Mikey, named after his late cousin Big Mike.

Kevin and René played a vital role in the day-to-day operations of the church. Together they handled the married couples' ministry. And after receiving his master's degree in divinity, Reverend Stokes promoted

Kevin to associate pastor. He had so much confidence in Kevin that every third Sunday of each month, he allowed him to deliver the morning sermon to the congregation.

Kevin and Reverend Stokes had grown extremely close over the years. Every day, he gave thanks to God for placing Reverend Stokes and his wife Gwendolyn in his life. Their presence had been critical to the success of his marriage and ministry. Kevin and Rená enjoyed many Saturday morning breakfasts with the Stokes, while sitting for hours listening to their shared wisdom.

In addition to the Saturday morning gatherings, every Wednesday, Kevin and Reverend Stokes met for lunch at Deacon Gilbert's soul food restaurant, located about two blocks from the church. But today was out of the ordinary. Reverend Stokes had called Kevin to meet for lunch on a Monday. He said he had something important to discuss.

**

"Good afternoon, André," Kevin greeted Deacon Gilbert by his first name as he stepped into the entrance of the restaurant.

"Hey, Kevin," Deacon Gilbert replied. "Reverend Stokes is waiting for you."

Kevin walked over to the table where his mentor sat. Reverend Stokes cordially stood up out his chair as Kevin approached. They shook hands, hugged, and took their seats.

"I took the liberty of ordering your usual fish and potato wedges," Reverend Stokes said.

"So, what's going on?" Kevin asked right away. He was curious. Today was the first time Reverend Stokes had ever called him off schedule for a lunch meeting.

"I got a call from Bishop Mathews last night. He is the overseer of our sister churches in Tennessee. He informed me that they have a vacant Pastor's position in his state," Reverend Stokes said.

"Okay, but I don't follow. What does that have to do with me?" Kevin asked suspiciously.

"The Bishop board has already voted to give the position to you. That's if you want it."

"No, I don't want it."

"How can you say no? You haven't even had time to think it over..." Reverend Stokes said before abruptly stopping mid-sentence. Deacon Gilbert's wife Angela interrupted them. She had their food in her hands.

"Good afternoon, Reverend Stokes... Minister Tyler," she formally greeted the two men. "I have fish and fries for you." She set a large plate of fried catfish fillets and potato wedges in front of Kevin. "...And I have steak and potatoes for you," she said to Reverend Stokes.

"Thank you, Sistah Angela. As always, the food looks delicious," Reverend Stokes said, complimenting her.

Kevin nodded his head with his mouth full of food. He couldn't say a word. As soon as Angela sat his plate down, he at once began devouring the freshly fried catfish.

"Thank you." She smiled shyly at the Reverend's praise. "Enjoy your lunch and if you two need anything else, just let me know," she said, and then turned and walked away.

Reverend Stokes smiled and chuckled as he and Kevin watched Angela strut back to the kitchen area.

"I can't help but smile every time I see her... I say to myself, that little woman's cooking must be something special." Reverend Stokes laughed.

Kevin smiled and nodded his head. He knew why Reverend Stokes was laughing. All the long-time church members knew the story. Angela and her four sisters had lived in Atlanta all their lives and had grown up in the church. About eighteen years ago, Deacon Gilbert, back then he was known simply as André, came to Atlanta from Ohio to visit his older brother John. John set him up on a blind date with Angela and André never left. The rumor around the church was that André had his mother sell his house back in Ohio and ship all his belongings to Atlanta. Since then, the single women in the church pay close attention to Angela and whisper among themselves that she must know the secret to nabbing a good man.

Reverend Stokes ate a few bites of food, before continuing his conversation. "How can you say no to this opportunity without thinking about it or even talking it over with your wife?"

Kevin hurried and finished chewing the food in his mouth. He swallowed hard and washed it down with a big gulp of ice-tea. "First of all, I don't want to leave Atlanta. Secondly, I'm not ready to be the pastor over my own congregation...Besides I'm comfortable right here with you."

"That's the answer I was looking for," Reverend Stokes said.

Kevin smiled. "So you agree that I shouldn't take the position."

"No, I think you should take it."

Kevin looked puzzled. "But you just said I gave you the answer you were looking for."

"You did give me the answer I was looking for. You said *you don't want* and *you're not ready*," Reverend Stokes replied, before putting his fork down and adjusting in his chair.

Kevin paid close attention to the Reverend's body language. He knew what was coming. *He's going into teach mode.*

Reverend Stokes looked directly into Kevin's eyes and said, "Most of the time, when God calls us to do something, it's something we *don't want* to do, and secondly, we are *never ready* to do God's work in our own strength.

"Please explain," Kevin said.

Reverend Stokes took a loud sip of ice-tea and continued teaching. "All men and women of God have a *ministry* and a *mission*. Our *ministry* is often tied to that God-given gift that we have from birth. It could be playing a sport, singing, preaching, leading, or any innate ability that God chooses to enhance and perfect within us. It has nothing to do with sin or your lifestyle.

"Romans 11:29 says, ...*For the gifts and callings of God come without repentance.* That scripture means that even before we repented of our sins, God's gifts are already present in us. Remember what God said to Jeremiah, before he was formed in his mother's womb he made him a prophet. Our gift and ministry have been in us all along. And because it has always been there, sometimes we take it for granted and begin operating in our own strength. And you know just as well as I do that we can't do anything for God in our own strength."

Kevin nodded his head in agreement and listened closely as Reverend Stokes continued to teach.

"If we think in our minds that we are ready to do God's work, that means we're confident in our own strength and abilities. However, if we do not believe we are ready and we decide to go forth anyway, that's when we learn to lean on God's strength to get us through. We learn to trust God more than we trust our own abilities. It takes courage to trust God to take us beyond what we know we can do."

"Whether I'm ready or not, I still *don't want* to leave Atlanta," Kevin interrupted.

"That's even more the reason why you should go," Reverend Stokes shot back at him.

"Why?" Kevin asked.

"Consider the prophets of the Bible," Reverend Stokes suggested. "Neither of them *wanted* to go when God called them for duty. Look at Moses for an example. He was living a comfortable life as a shepherd with a beautiful wife and two young sons. Going back to Egypt to face Pharaoh was the last thing he *wanted to do.* You know the story. Go to your Bible and read in Exodus, chapters 3 and 4. See how Moses responded when God told him to go back to Egypt. *Who am I to go unto Pharaoh...Lord, I am slow to speech...who shall I say sent me?* The man *did not want* to go, but he went anyway. He went in God's strength. That's why it was a successful mission."

Reverend Stokes paused for a second to allow Kevin a moment to process the message and then he continued to instruct. "But it doesn't stop with Moses. Go to the book of Judges, chapter 6, and read about Gideon. God had to prove to him by wetting and drying a fleece before he would go forth. And don't forget about poor Jonah, he had to spend three nights in the belly of a giant fish before he was willing to go. And then there is Jeremiah, Isaiah, the apostle Paul, and the list goes on and on of mighty men of God who *did not want* to go, but they *went* anyway. They went in God's strength."

"I understand what you're saying," Kevin said humbly.

"My advice to you is this. If God wants you to go, you go, but base your decision on God's will and not your own. You and Rená should pray about it. It's a good idea to seek God's counsel with your wife. God hears the prayers of a good wife," Reverend Stokes stated. "Now I'm going to finish eating before my food gets cold."

"Yes sir, I'll talk it over with Rená as soon as I get home."

Kevin smiled at the wise old man as he watched him consumed the rest of the steak and potatoes on his plate. He laughed to himself. Reverend Stokes looked like a six-foot-tall Poppa Smurf with his dark-complexion and snow-white beard. The truth was that he didn't want to leave his mentor. He always assumed he would take the helm at his church once Reverend Stokes retired or went home to glory. A strange church in a strange town in Tennessee was the last thing he expected for his life.

***

Chapter 6

"You may not have my last name nor my blood running through your veins, but you're my son in the gospel."

-Reverend Stokes

Kevin quietly entered Reverend Stokes' office and sat down on the plush leather couch.

Reverend Stokes remained seated behind his desk reading his Bible. He peeked up at Kevin and then fixed his eyes back on his Bible and continued reading.

"Is this the same sofa you had twenty years ago?" Kevin asked trying to start a conversation.

"No, it's not. I had it replaced about eight years ago," Reverend Stokes replied with a smirk. "I know you didn't interrupt my studies to ask me about that sofa." He closed his Bible, leaned back in his chair, and waited for Kevin's response.

"No, sir. I came to tell you face to face that I've talked it over with Rená and we have decided to take the position in Tennessee."

Reverend Stokes cracked a wide, teeth-showing smile at Kevin. "I already knew. Bishop Mathews called me this morning." He stood up and walked around his desk.

"Congratulations, Pastor Kevin Tyler," he said as he pulled Kevin up and gave him a big hug.

"Thank you, sir."

"So, what did your wife say when you told her about the offer?"

"Her exact words were, *I don't care if God called you to preach on the moon, I will happily go with you and support you one hundred percent.*"

"The Lord has blessed you with a good wife."

"She's truly a gift from God."

"So, when do you leave?"

"We leave next week. The church already has a house ready for us."

"Sit back down. I have something for you," Reverend Stokes said as he walked back around his desk. Opening a locked drawer, he pulled out a gift-wrapped box. "Here, this is for you." He handed the package to Kevin, who's eyes lit up. The box felt heavy.

"What is this?" He asked with a giant smile on his face.

"Open it," Reverend Stokes ordered. He sat down on the couch next to Kevin and watched as he unwrapped the gift.

Kevin quickly tore the wrap and opened the box. He hesitated before pulling it out of the box. It was a large black book with a soft leather cover and pages trimmed in gold. The book looked old. It reminded him of the *Book of Shadows* from the TV series *Charmed*. Written on the cover in large gold letters were the words, *The Pastor's*

Book of Warnings. He turned to Reverend Stokes. "What is this?"

"Open the book," Reverend Stokes instructed with a smile and a nod.

Kevin hesitated for a moment before carefully opening the book. He didn't want to tear any of the pages. The first page was a handwritten dedication page with names and dates, and written on the first line were the words, *Given to Nathaniel E. Stokes by Samuel L. Stokes, March 30, 1887.* Kevin read the line and then looked at Reverend Stokes, who smiled and gestured for him to continue reading. *Given to Joshua M. Stokes, April 25, 1917. Given to David L. Stokes, November 30, 1945. Given to Lawrence J. Stokes, August 23, 1978.* And written on the last line were the words, *Given to Kevin R. Tyler, January 18, 2023.*

"What's going on?" Kevin asked. "What is this?"

"It's *The Pastor's Book of Warnings.* It's filled with forewarnings, heeds, and woes that all pastors should be mindful of ...*especially new pastors...like you.*" Reverend Stokes emphasized. "My great-great-grandfather began writing in this book in 1860. He wrote in it for twenty-seven years before passing it down to his son, Nathaniel."

"Are you telling me this book is over one hundred and sixty years old," Kevin stated with amazement. "I can't accept this. This is a family heirloom. It's part of your family's legacy and belongs to your children."

"It belongs to a pastor," Reverend Stokes replied. "I'm getting old, and my children aren't preachers. You may not have my last name nor my blood running through your veins, but you're my son in the gospel. I birthed you and I trained and raised you in the ministry. I feel just as ccnfident giving this book to you as I would one of my children," he said to Kevin with sincerity in his voice.

Reverend Stokes' words touched Kevin. He couldn't turn the gift down. "Um...Thank you...I don't know what to say."

"You don't have to say anything, just accept the book and heed the warnings that are written inside."

Kevin carefully flipped through the pages. "There's so much in here, and why is it written in different handwriting?"

"Over the years, every pastor that has had this book has written in it. Whenever they would slip-up and fall into sin or hear of another preacher's shortcomings, they logged it into this book as a warning for future pastors to heed."

"Judging from the size of this book, there has been a lot of slip-ups and falls over the years," Kevin chuckled.

"No preacher is above reproach. Everyone makes mistakes, but the key is to admit your mistake, repent, learn from it and move on," Reverend Stokes advised.

"So, what did *you* write in here?" Kevin asked with a curious look on his face as he passed the book to his mentor.

Reverend Stokes paused for a moment. He grabbed the book out of Kevin's hand and began slowly flipping through the pages. When he finally stopped, he sat the open book down on his desk and told Kevin to read.

"Beware of the Pastor's burden..." Kevin read aloud. "What is the *Pastor's burden?*"

"The Pastor's burden is the burden you feel for the souls of God's people. It's when you desire to see them all saved and healed. You must possess this burden in your heart to be an effective Pastor."

"How is that a bad thing? This book says to beware of the *Pastor's burden.*"

"Yes, you do have to be careful. It is a good thing, and it's required of all pastors, but you can't let it overwhelm you. When you start neglecting your own house and begin doing any and everything for the people, that's when it becomes a problem," Reverend Stokes cautioned. "Always remember this, son. We may refer to them as our flock or our congregation, but they are God's people. I made the mistake of trying to save everybody. I did all I could for my flock. I was up at all times of the night, praying, loaning money, and giving all my time to the people. I was giving so much of my time that I didn't realize I was neglecting my wife and kids. They were suffering and I couldn't see it because of the burden I had for God's people."

"Isn't that just part of being a pastor? Sacrifices come with the job," Kevin said.

"You're right, we do have to make some sacrifices, but not our families. 1 Timothy 3:5 says, *for if a man knows not how to rule his own house, how shall he take care of the church of God.*"

"How did it affect your family?"

"First, my kids started acting out in school and then Gwen and I stopped spending quality time together. It had gotten so bad that she took the kids and filed for divorce."

Kevin burst out laughing. "You've got to be kidding. You and Mrs. Stokes are the perfect couple. I could never imagine her filing for divorce."

"It happened and if you're not careful, it can happen to you."

Kevin slowly nodded his head in agreement as he began flipping through the book again. "What does this entry mean, *Beware of Bathsheba...*? She wasn't a bad person"

"Obviously, you don't know that story as well as you think you do. You may have to go back and reread 2 Samuel Chapter 11," Reverend Stokes said.

"I know the story. King David seduced Bathsheba and after he got her pregnant, he had her husband murdered," Kevin said. "David was the one in the wrong."

"Yes, but he wasn't the only one," Reverend Stokes replied. He grabbed the open Bible off his desk and turned to 2 Samuel Chapter 11.

"Read verse two, and then ask yourself why Bathsheba was taking a bath outside, in the middle of the night. And if David could see her from the roof, it would make sense that she could see him too. She knew what she was doing out there. She wanted the king to see her beautiful body. Read on a little further and you will see that her husband was more dedicated to his job than he was to his wife, and it looks like she conspired with David to kill her husband to hide her pregnancy and cover up their sin. And even if you don't think she conspired with David to kill her husband, at the least, she knew about it, which made her complicit to the crime."

"Whoa, I've never looked at it from that angle. I guess a man should beware of a Bathsheba-type woman," Kevin stated.

Reverend Stokes laughed at him. "Just read the book and heed the warnings."

***

Chapter 7

And he gave some, apostles; and some, prophets; and some, evangelists; and some, pastors and teachers; For the perfecting of the saints, for the work of the ministry, for the edifying, of the body of Christ:

-Ephesians 4:11-12

"This is going to take some getting used to," Kevin said to Rená as he chauffeured his family through the narrow streets of Dyersburg.

A small industrial city in the northwest corner of Tennessee, Dyersburg had a population slightly over 17,000 people, with only twenty-five percent of it being African Americans, who largely populated the east and west sides of the city. Although considered contemporary because of its modern-day amenities, Dyersburg still maintained its small-town feel by remaining segregated just as it had in the 1950s.

Dyersburg had never had a black mayor, sheriff, or anyone of color that possessed any type of political power. Therefore, the black population of the city looked to the church for leadership in their community.

With over twenty churches serving more than 4,000 African Americans, many pastors exercised their influence throughout the community.

Kevin took over at New Hope Pentecostal Church. A two-hundred-member church located on the east side of town. He agreed to an annual salary of fifty thousand. He earned more than that in a month through his real estate investments. But Kevin was not financially motivated, he was following God's plan.

On Kevin's first Sunday as the pastor of New Hope Pentecostal Church, he felt a bit nervous. His family, mentors, and friends had all made the trip to Dyersburg in support of his inaugural day.

"Are you ready, Pastor Tyler?" Reverend Stokes asked as they sat in the Pastor's office moments before the morning service began.

"Yes sir." Kevin nervously nodded his head. "But before I go out there, would you please say a prayer for me?"

Reverend Stokes said a quick prayer and then Kevin stepped outside of his office and into the pulpit as the Pastor of New Hope Pentecostal Church.

****

Chapter 8

"Beware of the Damsel in distress..."

-The Pastor's Book of Warnings

It was 3:28 p.m. and April Dillon stood at her workstation at Dyersburg's Textiles. She eyed the clock on the wall waiting for it to hit 3:30. She was anxious to get off and take care of her business.

After a grueling eight-hour shift at the factory, she still had a busy afternoon ahead of her. Being a twenty-five-year-old single mother, she felt trapped, like the odds were stacked against her while trying to make ends meet—constantly on the move. Monday through Friday, April woke at 5:30 in the morning. After getting ready for work, feeding her four-year-old son, and dropping him off at daycare, she barely had enough time to make it to her job before seven.

"Finally, 3:30." April exhaled. She hurried to clock out and rushed out of the factory door. Once in the parking lot, she quickly scurried to her twelve-year-old Nissan Altima, jumped in, and with one hand on the steering wheel and the other on the key, she whispered a quick prayer before turning the ignition.

"Lord, please let this car start," she whispered with her eyes closed. For the past two years, April had been

41

whispering this little prayer every time she started her car.

Until two years ago, April never realized the value of having reliable transportation. But life had taught her a hard lesson. Not long ago, April struggled tremendously. Her car had broken down and she had to depend on the kindness of others to get to and from work, not to mention the fact she still had to pick her son up from daycare. All while listening to her mother's mouth whenever she helped.

April would never forget what she had to go through to get her car fixed. She had a bad alternator, and she couldn't afford a professional mechanic, so she allowed her landlord, Mr. Bud Hollingsworth to fix the car. He was a nasty, perverted old man in his mid-seventies. He was short and wrinkled, wore the same old dusty denim overalls and dirty cap every day and always reeked of motor oil. He had been sniffing around her ever since she moved into the duplex he owned. He would offer to pay her bills or give her free rent in exchange for sex. April would always turn him down gracefully. But when her car broke down, she had no choice but to give in and accept his proposition. It had been the nastiest and most embarrassing five minutes of her life and even though the incident happened over two years ago, she still cringed at the disgusting memory of Mr. Bud Hollingsworth on top of her.

Now that her car had been fixed, she made sure she kept the oil changed on time. She also remembered to get a yearly tune-up. She did, however, still whisper a quick prayer every time before turning the ignition.

After saying her prayer, the car started, and April cracked a smile. "Thank you, Jesus," she whispered.

In a hurry to pick up her son, CJ, from daycare, April sped through the mild Dyersburg traffic. She needed to feed him dinner and drop him off at her mother's house before heading to her night class at Dyersburg State Community College.

April had been a faithful member of New Hope Pentecostal Church for the past three years. She considered herself saved and fully sold out for the Lord, and not counting her disgusting ordeal with Mr. Bud, she had been celibate the entire time. She prayed daily that God would send her a good husband.

Lately, she had been working over-time on Saturdays to save money. Her goal was to save up enough money to attend the upcoming *Women Evolved* conference. She planned to go to the conference in Dallas and come back home on fire for God. She believed that if she could make it to the conference, God would bless her with a saved and sanctified husband that was fully committed to Jesus. April was focused and on a mission.

**

The sun shined bright as April walked calmly out of the church, holding her son's hand. CJ skipped playfully as she smiled. She was thinking about the sermon Pastor Tyler had just preached, *Stand still and Watch the Salvation of the Lord.* She loved the message. *It seemed like he was speaking directly to me"* she thought as she opened her car door and tickled CJ as she fastened him into his car seat. After buckling him in, April positioned herself behind the steering wheel, said her ritual prayer, and turned the ignition—but nothing happened. She closed her eyes, said another prayer, and timidly turned the ignition a second time, and again—nothing happened. Her car was dead.

"No, no. God please don't let this be happening to me again," she cried as she hit the steering wheel with the palm of her hand.

"What's wrong, Momma? Why you crying?"

"Nothing's wrong, baby. Momma is just a little upset that her car won't start," she said in an attempt to sound calm in front of her son. She was so upset when her car didn't start, she forgot he was in the backseat. But she had to keep it together for his sake. "C'mon, baby, let me get you out," she said as she reached down and popped the hood release before exiting the car. She unbuckled her son and helped him out. "Now stand next to momma," she ordered.

CJ quietly stood next to April as she looked under the hood of her car. April didn't know what she was doing or even what she was looking for. She just hoped and prayed someone would walk by and offer her some much-needed assistance.

Her prayers were answered when Deacon Bryce Jones and his wife Carmen walked through the church parking lot and noticed her hood propped up.

"Excuse me, Sistah April, do you need any help?" Deacon Jones asked.

"My car won't start. I think the battery might be dead."

"We can give you a boost," Carmen Jones suggested.

Deacon Jones pulled his Tahoe in front of April's Altima and connected the cable to the battery. After about fifteen minutes and a couple of tries, her car still wouldn't start. Now April was scared. She didn't know what to do. She felt helpless and embarrassed as she watched the other parishioners trickle out into the parking lot, get in their cars, and drive away. Deacon Jones and his wife were the only ones that stopped to help her.

The Deacon spent nearly half an hour investigating under the hood. He wasn't a professional mechanic, but he had worked on a few cars over the years. He knew enough to troubleshoot and figure out the most common car issues. "I think you're going to need a new alternator," he turned and said to April.

His words shot through April's ears like a sharp arrow. She instantly burst into tears as the memory of Mr. Bud flashed through her mind. Her body began to shake uncontrollably as she cried.

Kevin and Rená walked out of the church with their children. They heard April crying and walked over to see what was going on. Rená immediately put her arms around April in an attempt to comfort her.

Kevin asked Deacon Jones what the problem was. Deacon Jones explained the situation, Kevin didn't understand why April seemed so distraught. *Cars break down all the time.*

"You can leave now. Rená and I will handle it from here," Kevin said to Deacon Jones.

Carmen gave April a hug and a few words of encouragement before leaving.

"What can we do to help you?" Rená asked April as Kevin stood beside her and listened. He learned from

Reverend Stokes, always allow the First Lady to take the lead when dealing with female members.

"I'd appreciate it if you could give us a ride home. I'll just have to figure it out later," April muttered softly as she continued to cry.

"You don't have to cry, we can help you get your car fixed," Rená offered.

"Thank you, First Lady, I don't mean to cry like this. It's just that the last time my car broke down, I had so much trouble getting back and forth to work, and I had to beg people to pick my son up from daycare," April said as her crying gradually turned into soft sniffles.

Rená looked over at her brand-new Escalade parked in her personal parking space. She wanted to loan it to April, but she needed the space to haul *her* kids around town. Then she looked at Kevin's new Mercedes coupe parked next to hers. She had always felt God had blessed her family with way more than they needed. She never imagined herself as the type of First Lady that drove around in luxury vehicles while one of her members had to beg for a ride to work. *We have a BMW and a truck at home.* "You can take my husband's car," she suggested to April.

April looked at Kevin's Mercedes then bucked her eyes and shook her head at Rená. "No thank you, First Lady. I can't take the Pastor's car. If something happens, I can't afford to pay for no brand-new Benz."

Kevin was taken by surprise when Rená suggested April take his hundred-thousand-dollar car, but he loved his wife, and he knew she offered it from her heart. He couldn't go against her on this. He had to support her.

"It will be alright. It's just until we can get your car fixed," he insisted.

"Thank you. I promise I'll take care of it," April said.

April floated home in style in the Pastor's 2023 Mercedes S class. It was a completely different experience from her old run-down Altima. The interior was plush and elegant, and the soft leather and wood-grain finish made her feel like a million bucks. She was afraid to play with the car's touchscreen controls. She felt like she was in a spaceship. She pulled into the parking space at her little duplex apartment. She smiled as she sat in the car. She wished she could afford something this nice. She couldn't believe the First Lady trusted her with something so expensive. She wanted to drive all over Dyersburg, but for some strange reason, she was nervous. She didn't feel like she belonged in something so luxurious. As she sat parked in front of her apartment, she began looking around the car's interior and curiously opened the glove compartment.

"Oh!" She jumped when a bottle of Jimmy Choo cologne fell out. She opened it and sniffed the cap. "Mmm..." She smiled and moaned. "I see you, Pastor Tyler. No wonder you always smell so good," she said out loud as she examined the bottle. She thought about the times she heard women at church comment on how good the Pastor always smelled.

For the next five days, April drove back and forth to work in style. She loved driving the Pastor's Benz. She also got used to smelling his Jimmy Choo cologne. She could smell the scent every time she got inside the car. She even put a dab of it on the extra pillow in her bed. It felt good to have the scent of a man in the bed to curl up with at night. It made her pray even harder for God to send her a husband.

**

On Friday, Kevin and Rená pulled up at April's duplex in separate vehicles. Rená in her Escalade and Kevin drove April's newly repaired Altima. Kevin remained silent while Rená explained to April that her car had been repaired and the maintenance bill was all taken care of. She didn't have to pay anything.

"Thank you so much, First Lady," April said as she hugged Rená. "And thank you, Pastor Tyler." She smiled.

Kevin nodded and smiled as well. He was proud of his wife for helping a young member in need.

"Before we go, I noticed you didn't sign your son up for Kid's Day tomorrow," Rená said.

"I wanted to, but I have to work overtime tomorrow," April replied.

"He can go with us. Kevin and I will take care of him," Rená suggested.

"You've done more than enough for me by fixing my car. I don't want to impose on you any more than I already have," April said.

"It's not a problem. I think it would be fun for CJ to experience Kid's Day with the other children in the church," Rená insisted. "Pack his things. He can spend tonight with us. We'll take good care of him and I'll bring him home tomorrow evening as soon as everything is over."

"Do you want to come with me?" Kevin asked CJ and then picked him up.

"Yes." CJ nodded shyly while looking at his mother for approval.

April looked at her son as the Pastor held him in his arms. The sight saddened her. She felt bad that her son didn't have a father in his life. Seeing him happy and content in the Pastor's arms touched her, so she allowed him to go with them. *He deserves to have fun,* she reasoned to herself.

Later that night, while in bed, she cried and prayed for God to send her a husband, not only for her but also for her child's sake.

****

Chapter 9

"She needs me, it's my duty as her Pastor to fulfill her needs."

-Pastor Tyler

Kid's Day was a blast. CJ had so much fun. Kevin felt proud as he watched his wife with all the kids. Rená loved kids, and if it were up to her, they would have a house full. But after God blessed them with a boy and a girl, Kevin begged her to get her tubes tied. He loved kids too, but he wasn't interested in raising a basketball team.

The day was going perfect until the end of the evening when Kevin's daughter, Joann, had an emergency. She wore white shorts and didn't realize that she had gotten her first period. Of course, when she did notice, she became extremely embarrassed and started to cry. Rená took Joann and Little Mikey home. So, she asked Kevin to drop off CJ in her absence.

Kevin faithfully followed Rená's instructions and drove CJ home. By the time he pulled up to April's apartment, CJ had fallen asleep. Kevin grabbed the bag of toys and candy CJ had won at the picnic. He picked the little boy up in his arms, carried him to the door, and pressed the doorbell.

Expecting her First Lady, April answered the door wearing nothing but a long nightshirt and panties. "Oh, Pastor..." April sounded startled. "Where is First Lady?"

"Shh...he's asleep," Kevin whispered. "Where is his bedroom?"

"Follow me," April whispered back and motioned for him to follow her. She led him to the entrance of CJ's bedroom.

She smiled as Kevin walked past her with her son sound asleep in his arms. He carried CJ to his room and laid him down on his bed. His experience as a father of two kicked in and he instinctively took CJ's shoes and socks off and snugged him under the covers.

April stood at the door and watched as Kevin tucked her son in bed. Tears trickled out of her eyes. She felt guilty and silently blamed herself for not having a male figure in her son's life.

As Kevin walked toward the door of the bedroom, he couldn't help but noticed how the hallway light exposed the silhouette of April's body through her thin nightshirt. He quickly shook it off and tried to hurry past her, but he saw the tears running down her cheeks.

"What's wrong, Sistah April? Why are you crying?"

"It's nothing, Pastor." She lowered her head and quickly wiped her tears.

"It has to be something. Nobody cries for nothing," he said gently.

"I just feel like it's my fault that my son doesn't have a father figure in his life." Her voice quivered as tears continued to trail down her face.

Kevin's instinct as a pastor was to comfort her, so without thinking, he opened his arms to offer her a hug.

April leaned her head into his chest, and gently wrapped her arms around him and squeezed. And in an instant, she was comforted. She felt safe and relaxed in his arms. She closed her eyes and took a deep breath. But at that moment, something unexpected happened. April was aroused by the scent of his cologne, and a tingling sensation simmered between her legs. She took another deep breath and considered her dilemma. She weighed her options in her head. Should she keep holding on to him, or should she let go and escort him to the door? *It wouldn't be right to make a pass at my pastor,"* she thought... but she didn't let go.

Kevin held April in his arms and comforted her as a father would a crying daughter. He didn't think anything of it, because right then, he was just a pastor, consoling one of his members. The embrace seemed innocent...until he realized how tight she had her body pressed against him and how her arms were wrapped a little too snug around his torso. He felt the fullness of her breast next to his body.

She needs more comforting. What can I do to make her feel better?

The longer and tighter April held him, the more he felt she needed him. Compelled to comfort her even more, he gave her a soft kiss on the forehead and held her a little tighter in his arms.

Electricity shot through April's body when his lips touched her forehead. She looked up into his eyes and saw what she needed in a man. She felt safe and whole in his arms, like this was where she belonged, wrapped securely in his embrace. *Lord, forgive me for what I'm about to do.* She stood on her toes, and kissed him on his lips.

Kevin knew what she did was wrong, but he didn't even try to fight it. It felt too good. It felt so natural, that he kissed her back.

Damn, Kevin. What are you doing? he thought as he felt April's tongue slide inside his mouth. *She needs me. It's my duty as her Pastor to fulfill her needs.* He tried to justify his actions.

Kevin opened his mouth and kissed April with every ounce of passion in his body. He reached down, grabbed her firm butt cheeks, and lifted her off the floor.

April wrapped her legs around his waist as he pinned her against the wall. They kissed feverishly as they squeezed and pressed their bodies together. They sounded like two panting dogs as their breathing became loud and erratic. Kevin walked her through the hallway of her tiny apartment, and with aggressive passion, he threw her down on her living room sofa and quickly pulled his shirt off while she wildly tried to unbuckle his pants.

By now, they were too far gone to stop. Both consumed with lust. All Kevin could think about was getting his pants down so he could plunge deep in April's hot flesh, and April's body craved to feel him inside of her.

With his help, April finally managed to unbuckle his pants and gasped at the sight of his exposed manhood. "Oh, Pastor," she sighed through heavy breaths. She hadn't seen a penis in years, especially one that size. She burned with lust, and his fully erect shaft looked so tantalizing to her that she couldn't control her urges and without giving it a second thought, she took him into her mouth.

"AHH..." Kevin moaned as he felt the warmth of April's mouth wrapped around his manhood, a feeling he hadn't felt since before he was married. Rená had been in church all her life and didn't approve of oral sex. She would often say to him, "A man's penis does not belong in a woman's mouth, or God didn't intend for people to have oral sex."

The sensation of April's oral stimulation was too much for Kevin to handle. He exploded in less than a minute.

"Mmm..." April moaned as she drained her pastor of his manly nectar. Now she was really on fire. She slowly released him from her oral grip and pulled her shirt over her head to lay back on the couch.

Caught up in the moment, Kevin ripped her panties off, eager to return the favor. His mouth salivated at the thought of tasting her flesh. He hadn't tasted a woman's sweetness since before he was married.

Kevin hungrily dove face first between April's legs, licking, sucking, and bringing her to a much-needed orgasm.

"Wait," April whined after her orgasm, her voice trembling. "Let's go to my bedroom." She grabbed Kevin's hand and led him to her bed. A quickie on her living room sofa just wasn't going to do. Now that she had crossed the line with her handsome well-endowed pastor, she wanted more. She needed to feel his body on top of hers, making love to her in bed just like a husband would make love to his wife. She laid back on the bed, allowing him to sensually caress every part of her body. He tenderly kissed each of her soft mounds and prepared to enter her sacred temple, when she stopped him. She looked into his eyes and whispered, "Take it slow, I haven't been with a man in over three years." She closed her eyes and submitted to whatever type of passion her pastor was willing to give.

****

Chapter 10

"I tried to call your cellphone."

-Rená Tyler

For over a half-an-hour, Kevin sat in his driveway looking up at his bedroom window. He didn't know what to do. His conscience was drenched with guilt and his body carried the scent of another woman. From where he parked, he could see the lamplight was still on in his bedroom, which meant Rená had waited up for him.

Kevin quietly entered his house with the guilt of having sex with April on his shoulders. He felt like he weighed a thousand pounds as he slowly inched up the stairs to his bedroom. He carefully eased the door open, hoping Rená had fallen asleep with the lamp on. But he wasn't that fortunate. She was propped up in bed watching a Tubi movie.

"Hey, honey." She looked up and greeted him. "What took you so long?"

"I had to stop by the church on my way home," Kevin replied. *I can't believe I just lied to my wife.* He turned his head, careful not to make eye contact with her.

"I tried to call you on your cellphone," she added.

"Uh…yeah. I left it in the car," he said and then hastily made his way to the master bathroom.

Rená's womanly intuition suddenly kicked in, and she instantly sprung out of bed and followed him to the bathroom. In their seventeen years of marriage, she had seen every facial expression he had, and she could hear in his voice and see in his countenance something wasn't right.

"Kevin, what's wrong?" She raised her voice as she grabbed his arm.

Kevin's initial reaction was to get defensive with her, until he looked into her face. She didn't show a hint of suspicion. He only saw love and concern in her eyes.

"Nothing's wrong, sweetheart. The Lord has just dropped something heavy in my spirit for tomorrow's sermon and I have a lot of work to do tonight." *Now I have just lied on God.* He swallowed the lump in his throat and his stomach turned as guilt continued to flood his conscience.

"I stayed up and waited for you so we could spend some quality time together," she said with a touch of sadness in her voice. Quality time was her way of saying she wanted to make love. "But I don't want to get in the way of God's voice. Don't stay up too late. Goodnight honey…I love you." She gave him a quick peck on the lips, turned off the lamp, and crawled back in bed.

After taking a long hot shower, Kevin spent the rest of the night crying and praying for forgiveness in his downstairs office.

****

Chapter 11

"No, I'm alone. Rená drove the kids to Atlanta for the weekend."

-Pastor Tyler

Three weeks had gone by since Kevin's indiscretion with April. He had been trying to put that night behind him and move on with his life, but he couldn't seem to shake the feelings of guilt and unrighteousness. It haunted him to his soul. It had even affected his preaching. He hadn't been able to muster up an original sermon. The previous Sunday, he preached a recycled version of a sermon Reverend Stokes delivered five years ago. Kevin felt he had become deaf to God's voice.

Earlier that morning, Rená drove the kids to Atlanta. The baby shower for her sister was the following day, and she wanted to make sure to be there in enough time to help with the finishing touches. Since they wouldn't be returning until late Sunday evening, Kevin intended to fully take advantage of his weekend of solitude. He planned on spending Friday night watching Creflo Dollar and T.D. Jakes' sermons. Saturday would be a day of fasting and prayer. However, before his weekend could officially begin, he needed to make a quick trip to Wal-Mart for supplies.

The store was more crowded than usual, which was typical for a Friday evening in Dyersburg, but it didn't bother Kevin. He just wanted to hurry up and snatch his items so he could go home and relax. But as he stood in the aisle looking at the different lavender-scented candles, he felt some tiny arms grab his leg.

"Oh!" A startled Kevin jumped. He looked down and April's son CJ had his leg in a bear hug.

"Hey, little man. Where did you come from?" Kevin reached down and picked the child up in his arms.

CJ smiled and pointed at April, who was walking hastily toward them with an angry expression on her face.

"I told you not to run off from me," she fussed at her son. "I'm sorry, Pastor Tyler. He saw you standing over here and he just took off running."

"It's okay," Kevin assured her as he turned his attention to CJ in his arms. "You need to listen to your mother. Don't run away from her when you're in the store. Okay?" Kevin said with gentle authority.

With his finger in his mouth, CJ nodded his head.

"Now, tell her you're sorry," Kevin ordered.

CJ looked at his mother. "I sorry," he said softly.

April's face lit up. She loved the chemistry between CJ and her pastor.

Kevin put CJ down, and he quickly ran to his mother, grabbed her hand, and stood obediently beside her as if he was trying to please the pastor.

Kevin and April stared at each other with an uncomfortable, guilty silence looming in the air between them. They hadn't spoken to each other since the night they'd made love, and now because of CJ, they had finally come face to face.

Kevin went first to break the strange morning-after vibe between them. "How have you been? Have you had any more problems with your car?" he asked awkwardly.

"Everything has been good. I haven't had any problems." April smiled and batted her eyes, signaling to him that she was okay with what had happened between them.

The image of her firm naked body flashed through his head. He tried to ignore it, but he couldn't. "That's good. Rená will be happy to know that everything is well with you," he said in a futile attempt to invoke his wife's name as if it would magically ward off the lustful desires he felt toward April.

"Is she here with you?" April inquired.

"No, I'm alone. Rená drove the kids to Atlanta for the weekend," Kevin said. His eyes surveying her body, he unconsciously wet his lips, and in a guilty coded message, he telepathically conveyed, *I will be alone and available for the entire weekend.*

"Oh...Uh...Okay." April hesitated in her response. The shift in her eyes and the vibration of her voice told Kevin that she understood the unspoken message he sent her. "So, what are the candles for?" she asked while looking in the blue Wal-Mart basket he held in his hand.

"These are scented candles. They're good for relaxing and meditating," he replied.

"Do they work?"

"Yes, I use them all the time," he said.

"I think I'll buy a couple of them for myself," she said, grabbing two lavender-scented candles off the shelf. "I'm going to put CJ to bed at about 9 o'clock tonight, and then I'm going to burn one of these candles while I take a bubble bath." She smiled as she played with her hair and looked Kevin up and down. Now she was the one sending a coded message. *I will be ready for you tonight after 9 p.m.*

"It sounds like you have your night all planned out," he replied with a devilish grin. The look in his eyes confirming tonight's secret tryst.

April said her goodbyes, and then she turned and walked away with a smirk on her face and an extra sway in her hips.

Later that night, at around 9:15, April's doorbell rang. She had been waiting for her Pastor. She opened the door and greeted him with a kiss.

****

Chapter 12

"Beware of the spirit of Bathsheba..."

-The Pastor's Book of Warnings

Carmen Jones tossed her leather Louis Vuitton gym bag onto the backseat of her Cadillac XT5. She was a successful real estate agent as well as the wife of Deacon Bryce Jones. Tonight, she filled in as a cycling instructor at her brother's fitness gym. She loved to work out. Her body was one of her biggest obsessions, and she worked extra hard to maintain her astonishing figure. Her generous, six-figure income allowed her the flexibility she needed to pamper herself and to be afforded with the finest designer clothes. On the surface, she appeared to be a good girl, but she was far from it. Carmen had a carnal itch hidden deep inside her flesh, and it was an itch that her husband could never seem to scratch.

Carmen and Bryce were both forty and they had been married for fifteen years. Together, they'd created two beautiful daughters, twelve-year-old Carla and ten-year-old Lisa. Bryce and Carmen were high school sweethearts, but after graduation, their lives went in different directions. Bryce accepted a scholarship to play football at the University of Tennessee at Martin and

Carmen attended Tennessee State University in Nashville.

While in college, Bryce was an active member of a local church, and he led his football team in prayer before each game. After completing six years of college, he graduated with a master's degree in education. Currently, Bryce worked as a football coach and history teacher at Dyersburg High School.

Carmen had always been one of the popular, pretty girls in high school. An honor student and cheerleader, she was thought to be the perfect princess. Bryce was an All-American, high school star football player. He was her smart and safe choice for a boyfriend.

But everything changed for Carmen when she went away to college. TSU was a completely different environment from small-town Dyersburg. Everything seemed to move so fast for her in college. The parties, the boys, along with sex and alcohol, mixed with a lack of supervision was too much for a small-town first-year student to handle.

College allowed Carmen the freedom to explore certain behaviors that she had never been privileged to experience before. She developed an insatiable appetite for bad boys, and gangbangers. High-rolling drug dealers peaked at the top of her list. Wild nights, loads of drugs, and poor judgment eventually led Carmen on the roller coaster ride that began her promiscuous double life.

While in college, she had two secret abortions, and she experienced a few bouts with gonorrhea. And after six wild years of college, she barely managed to graduate with a bachelor's degree in business management.

After college, Carmen and Bryce returned to Dyersburg where they reconnected, and again, Bryce was her smart and safe choice for a husband. No one in Dyersburg was aware of her adventurous college years, which made her the perfect catch for Bryce.

In the beginning, married life was good to Carmen, that was until the birth of her second child. After Lisa was born, the bad-boy urges seemed to resurface. She craved a little more excitement in her life. She loved her husband, and she never planned to divorce him, but he just wasn't fulfilling her sexual needs. Bryce was handsome, smart, and packing enough downstairs to please about any woman, but to Carmen, he was weak, boring, and too gullible. He never raised his voice or showed any kind of strong emotions. He believed anything she said, and he never got jealous. Carmen hated it. She always wondered how such a perfect man could be so boring.

Of course, Bryce's boring personality echoed into their sex life. He was so predictable that Carmen knew exactly how long he would last in each position. Some nights she would peek over at the digital clock on their nightstand and time him. In missionary style, he could last up to six minutes. In doggystyle, he would only last for three, and he would barely make it for two minutes if she got on top. Even after fifteen years of marriage, he still couldn't bring her to an orgasm. Some nights, after sex, she would sneak to the bathroom downstairs and masturbate while fantasizing about one of her college boyfriends. Over the years, Bryce had let himself go. His once muscular physique was now fat and flabby. This only added to Carmen's frustration. She felt that if she was willing to work hard on her body, he should too.

Throughout her marriage, Carmen had cheated on Bryce multiple times, but of course, he was clueless. He was either busy with coaching or helping at church that he didn't pay much attention to the things she did. No matter how late she came home at night, all she had to say was, "I had to work late," or "My brother needed help at the gym," and Bryce wouldn't ask any questions.

**

From the first moment Carmen laid eyes on Pastor Tyler at his formal meet and greet, she knew she had to have him. The Pastor's title didn't fool her. She could see the ex-bad boy swag written all over him. She eyed the $3,500 corduroy Tom Ford blazer he was wearing, and she was impressed when she peeked down and noticed the $1400 Christian Louboutin boots, he had on. *Oh yeah, this ain't no average pastor.*

When she finally introduced herself to him, she smelled the alluring scent of his Jimmy Choo cologne. "Humph," she smirked. She recognized the scent, because she had bought Bryce a bottle for his last birthday, and he had only worn it once. *His boring ass is still stuck on Cool Water,* she thought as she cut her eyes and rolled them at her husband.

After meeting the new pastor, Carmen decided to check out his wife to scrutinize her competition. She politely introduced herself to First Lady Rená Tyler. The two women had a brief but very informative conversation. Carmen found out that Pastor Tyler was also into real estate. She noted the similarities in their ages and the ages of their children, and since they shared so much in common, Carmen suggested to Rená that she and Bryce be their host family to the city. Rená liked the idea and accepted an invitation to have dinner with the deacon's family.

Carmen wasn't impressed nor intimidated by the First Lady. *She's pretty, but she's not sexy.* She could also see that Rená was a bit square and prudish. In college, she used to call girls like Rená *delicate little flowers.* She knew Rená's sexual talents were inferior to hers. *A delicate flower can never fully satisfy a bad boy.* She smirked as she sipped on a glass of punch, while lustfully cutting her eyes at her new pastor. She was like a hungry wolf, licking her chops at her unsuspecting prey.

****

Chapter 13

"Whoa, Sistah Jones. What are you doing?"

-Pastor Tyler

Carmen made sure her family spent as much time as possible with the Tyler's. They ate dinner together, went out on family bowling nights and their daughters had regular sleepovers. Their families were getting along well and growing close. Kevin and Bryce had even become best friends.

Carmen tried to use their friendship to talk Kevin into investing in a piece of industrial property, but he wasn't interested in investing in anything in Dyersburg. After weeks of trying, Carmen whispered to Rená about it, and she persuaded Kevin to meet with Carmen and listen to her proposal.

Kevin agreed to meet at her downtown office. But when he arrived, the door was locked. He took a step back to reread the sign on the door. "Carmen Jones Realty," he read aloud. He gently pecked on the glass door with his key chain. Carmen appeared from a room in the back. She waved and motioned for him to come in. Kevin pulled on the handle and pointed. She hurried to the door once she realized it was locked.

"I'm sorry, Pastor. My secretary must have locked the door when she left earlier."

"This place is nice," he said as he looked around, admiring the décor.

"Thank you." She sneakily locked the door back. "My office is back here." She motioned for him to follow her.

"I apologize again for the locked door. My secretary got off at five o'clock. I guess she locked it out of habit."

"It's okay," Kevin said as they walked into her back office. "Now *this* is a nice setup," he complimented her.

"Have a seat."

Kevin looked around. He didn't know whether to sit in one of the chairs in front of her desk or on the white leather couch against the wall, so he remained standing.

Carmen picked up two folders off her desk. "Take a look at this," she said as she sat down on the couch.

Kevin sat down next to her and listened to her presentation. After about ten minutes, she stopped and offered him a drink.

"Would you like some apple or grape juice?" she asked as she got up and opened the mini refrigerator behind her desk.

"No, thank you. I'm good," Kevin said, concentrating on the papers in his hand.

Carmen took a sip of her apple juice then stood and watched Kevin as he reviewed the documents. "I need to ask you a question," Carmen said with a conniving look in her eyes.

Kevin didn't detect the subtle change in her voice. His mind was more focused on the papers in front of him. "Sure, go ahead."

"Now keep this between the two of us," Carmen said.

"Okay," Kevin replied.

"Do you think my husband is uh...uh... gay?" she asked slyly.

"GAY!" Kevin's voice shrieked. "Nooo... Sistah Carmen. I don't think Deacon Jones is gay. Why would you ask me a question like that?"

"I don't know." She grimaced pretending to be uncomfortable with the subject. "It's just that he doesn't touch me like he used to."

"I can't speak on how he touches you, but I don't believe it's because he's gay."

"To be honest with you, Pastor, he has never really touched me the way I wanted him to." She pouted.

"Wait a minute, Sistah Jones. I don't think you should be talking to me about this."

"Why shouldn't I? You're my pastor. Who else should I talk to about it?"

"My wife... You should talk to Rená about this."

"I don't want another woman to know my husband isn't satisfying me. That's embarrassing," she frowned at him.

Kevin didn't know how to respond to her last statement. He didn't say a word. He just sat there on the couch with a confused look on his face.

"Do you think something's wrong with me?" she asked. Now pretending to sound insecure.

"I don't understand the question," he replied.

"I mean the way I look—my body."

"Oh, no, Sistah Carmen, you're beautiful. I think you look amazing."

"Thank you, Pastor. I work hard trying to keep my body in shape," she said as she turned her back to him and began unbuttoning her shirt without him noticing. "How can you say I look amazing when you haven't even seen what my body looks like?" And without warning, she turned back around with her shirt wide open, giving him a peek at her sexy bronze six-pack, and then she slid her shirt off her shoulders, showing her perky grapefruit-size breast.

"Whoa, Sistah Jones. What are you doing?" Kevin quickly jumped to his feet.

"I want you to see me the way my husband sees me," she said as she calmly reached behind her waist and unzipped her skirt, allowing it to drop to her feet. Then she slowly stepped to the side, leaving her skirt laying on the floor beside her.

Kevin stood frozen with his mouth hung open. She wasn't wearing any panties, and he was unable to take his eyes off her perfectly sculptured body. She unfastened her bra and tossed it on her desk and did a seductive pirouette in her heels to allow him a panoramic view of her sexiness.

"Now, what do you think?" she asked with a devilish smile on her face as she stood in front of him with nothing but her heels on.

71

Kevin took a deep breath. He couldn't believe what was happening. *This is wrong.* Yet he couldn't resist the temptation to enter such an attractive piece of flesh. With his conscience already sullied from his ongoing affair with April, Kevin reasoned that since he was already wallowing in adultery, one more act of sinful pleasure wouldn't make much difference and without any further resistance, he surrendered to the moment.

****

Chapter 14

"Now come on and sign this contract."

-Carmen Jones

Deacon Jones' daughter Carla had invited little Mikey and Joann to her pool party to celebrate her thirteenth birthday. Deacon Jones asked Kevin and Rená to come along and act as chaperones.

Kevin and his family pulled up in front of the Jones' house. He felt uncomfortable. The gathering was the first time he'd visited their home since having sex with Carmen. It had been two weeks since he and Carmen began their affair, and he had made four more evening visits to her office since the first day.

Kevin walked out to the pool area and noticed Carmen had her "perfect wife" face on. She was dressed down from her normal attire, without makeup or heels. She simply wore an orange and yellow sundress with sandals, but he couldn't keep his eyes off her. He knew what her body really looked like underneath that dress.

Carmen noticed Kevin's eyes constantly drifted in her direction. She winked and smiled every time she caught his lust-filled gaze. Bryce never looked at her like that and she was turned on. So much so that she decided to play a risky game.

"You know Pastor Tyler and I have closed the deal on that industrial property we've been looking at," she said to Rená in the presence of the rest of the adults.

"That's good, girl," Rená said, and she turned to Kevin and playfully popped him on his arm. "Kevin, why didn't you tell me you and Carmen had closed on that deal?"

"Uhh...I was waiting until I signed the contracts," he gave Carmen a puzzling look.

"That reminds me, I have the contracts in my briefcase in the house. You can sign them right now instead of driving to my office," Carmen suggested.

"Yeah, baby. Go ahead and sign them now," Rená insisted.

"C'mon, the papers are in here," Carmen motioned for Kevin to follow her inside the house.

He followed her upstairs to her bedroom and watched as she peeked out of the window.

"Come over here and look at this view."

Kevin looked out of the window. "This is a great view. I can see the entire pool area from here."

"Exactly!" she said excitedly. She pushed him out of the way, pulled her panties down to her knees, and raised her dress above her waist. And while holding her dress with one hand, she bent over and peeked out of the window. "C'mon, Pastor, hurry up and give me some," she said while patting her naked butt cheek and motioning for him to get behind her.

"Are you crazy?" he whispered loud and nervously. "My wife and your husband are down there, not to mention the other adults and our kids too."

"I know," she said with her devilish smile. "I can see everybody from right here. I'll know if someone is coming, we ain't gonna get caught...Now come on and sign this contract." She turned back around and peeked through the blinds.

Kevin paused for a second to admire her perfectly round apple bottom, and then he eased behind her and gave her what she wanted.

In less than ten minutes, they returned to the pool area. No one noticed that they were sweating, and their faces were flushed red. Neither Kevin or Carmen bothered to wash up or even wipe down. Both returned still wet with each other's juices and for the rest of the party, they smiled and made eyes at each other as they felt the high of their risky sexual escapade.

*****

Chapter 15

"Beware of the spirit of the Lonely Widow..."

-The Pastor's Book of Warnings

Cindy McGuire stood quietly in the back of the church and listened to the new Pastor deliver his sermon. At age sixty-five, she was one of the church's oldest members. She had been a member of New Hope Pentecostal Church for nearly forty years, and for twenty of those years, she had faithfully carried out her duties as the head usher.

Sunday after Sunday, she dutifully adorned herself in her pristine white uniform. With a simple nod of her head and a subtle motion of her powerful white gloves, she exercised her authority without saying a word. Her matching pearl necklace and earrings added a touch of class to her Sunday morning ensemble. She was five-feet-ten inches tall, slender, with long thick white hair. A former classical dance instructor, Cindy walked and stood with perfect poise and posture.

Over the years, she had become a part of the church's fixture. She never missed Sunday service and served three pastors during her tenure as head usher. Cindy's motto had always been the same. Remain in your seats, keep quiet, little girls should act like ladies and little boys should act like gentlemen. Everyone called her Ms. Cindy.

Born and raised in Dyersburg, Cindy attended college at Fisk University in Nashville, where she studied music and classical dance. While at Fisk, she met her husband, Carl McGuire. After graduating from college, they got married, moved to Dyersburg, and had a daughter. Fifteen years ago, Carl died suddenly of a brain aneurysm, leaving Cindy devastated. Later that same year, her daughter moved away to attend Spellman College in Atlanta.

After the loss of her husband, and departure of her daughter, Cindy struggled with depression. She eventually retired from teaching and became isolated and withdrawn. She vowed never to remarry nor date another man. *I'm too old to train another man* or *Jesus is the only man I need,* she would declare to anyone that questioned her, but deep down she felt lonely.

Cindy tried staying busy to cope. She had immersed herself in the church and taught music for free. Volunteering at all the church's events and Bible study often helped with the loneliness.

Her daughter was now married with three children and lived in Arizona. She tried convincing Cindy to move and help with the grandkids, but Cindy didn't want to live in Arizona. She believed her purpose was at New Hope Pentecostal church.

Cindy still exercised most days, which is how she maintained her dancer's body. She loved jogging and yoga, which always kept her mind occupied. The torture of being alone often kicked in at night. Some nights, when she missed her husband, she would dress in an evening gown and pretend to dance with him in front of the mirror.

Over the years since her husband has passed, Cindy had secretly developed a voracious appetite for watching porn while masturbating. It helped her cope with her sexual urges. She believed that as long as she did it by herself in the privacy of her own home, it was all right with God. She'd even ordered a few sex toys online. She was excited when she realized she could order a toy the same size and skin tone as her late husband.

***

The church's secretary, Jackie Lawrence, has botched the order for the new usher uniforms. She had mistakenly ordered black uniforms instead of the traditional white. And because Ms. Cindy is the head usher, the order had been sent directly to her house.

Kevin had to drive across town in pouring rain to Ms. Cindy's house to pick up the messed-up order. This had completely ruined his plans. Today was the only day this week he could meet Carmen at her office. And now, because of Jackie's mistake, he would have to wait until next week to enjoy the gratifying pleasures of her flesh.

Kevin pulled into Ms. Cindy's driveway. He got out of his car, opened his umbrella, and sprinted to her door. He was careful not to get his $300 Dyne jogging suit wet. He wore it especially for his meeting with Carmen. He wanted easy access to her stolen waters.

Ms. Cindy was running on her treadmill when she heard the knock at the door. She had been up late the night before dealing with her loneliness. She woke up this afternoon and decided to exercise to release some of her frustrations.

When Ms. Cindy opened the door, Kevin noticed she was drenched in sweat and wearing a mid-cut halter-top with black spandex tights.

"Hey, Pastor Tyler. How are you doing?" she said with a confused look on her face as she tried to catch her breath. She was surprised to see him. He had never been to her house before.

Kevin hesitated when she opened the door. "Ms. Cindy!" he blurted out. He was startled by how beautiful she looked. He had never seen her without her glasses, and she looked so much younger with her hair pulled back into a ponytail.

"Don't just stand out there in the rain, come in." She smiled.

"Oh, I'm sorry." He apologized for staring at her. "I almost didn't recognize you without your glasses," he commented nervously, and then his eyes skimmed over her body and paused for a moment at the obvious camel toe pressing through her spandex tights.

Ms. Cindy noticed his eyes checking her out, but she wasn't offended. She was flattered to know her body could still demand the attention of a much younger man. Besides, she would never wear her tights in public.

"What brings you by?" she asked.

Her question snapped him out of his daze. "The uniforms...Jackie told me about the mix-up," he said. "Please tell me Jackie called and told you I was on my way."

"She did call, but she didn't say anything about you coming by."

"I'm sorry Ms. Cindy. Please forgive me for dropping by unannounced." Kevin apologized again. "There must have been some sort of miscommunication between Sistah Jackie and me. I thought she informed you that I was coming over to get the uniforms."

"It's alright, Pastor," she assured him. "Here, the uniforms are right over there," she said as she directed his attention to a large box in her living room.

Ms. Cindy stood over Kevin with her hands on her hips as he examined the contents of the box. He couldn't help but think about how attractive she looked to him and now that she stood over him, her pronounced camel toe was directly in his face.

"Are the sizes correct?" he asked as he tried not to focus on her body.

"Yes."

"So, it's just the color that's wrong?"

She nodded. "Yes."

"I'll have to send them all back. Do you have the invoice?" he asked.

"Yes, I think it's back here in my bedroom. I'll get it. Here is the remote control for the TV. Have a seat and make yourself at home," she said, and then turned and walked out of the living room.

"Wow," Kevin said under his breath as he watched her walk away. Her butt was round, and firm and she moved like a teenager in her cute little Nike running shoes. It was hard to believe she was in her sixties.

Kevin took a seat on her couch and decided to turn on CNN to see what was going on in Trump news, but when he turned on the television, a porn movie popped up on the screen. "Whoa..." Kevin said.

As soon as Cindy picked the invoice up off her dresser, it dawned on her that her TV was still set on the movie she had been watching the night before. "Oh no," she gasped, before rushing back into her living room to stop him before he turned on the TV, but she was too late. She halted in her tracks when she saw him watching the movie from last night.

Their eyes meet when she entered the room.

"Forgive me, Pastor Tyler. I'm so sorry you had to see that. I didn't realize it was still on...I was..." She tried to explain but Kevin cut her off.

"Listen, Ms. Cindy, whatever you do in the privacy of your own home is your business."

"But I'm sorry, Pastor..."

"You don't have to keep apologizing to me. I'm not going to judge you on this. I don't have a heaven or a hell to put you in."

Cindy stood silent with an embarrassed look on her face.

"Is that the invoice?" Kevin asked, pointing at the piece of paper in her hand.

"Oh, yes," she said.

Kevin stood when she gave him the piece of paper. As he read over the invoice, he sensed a strange silence from Ms. Cindy. He took his eyes off the paper and peeked over at her. Something held her attention. He noticed her gaze was focused downward. He didn't realize what she was staring at so hard until he followed her eyes. She was looking down towards his midsection with her eyes locked on the erection bulging through his jogging pants. She looked up at him just as he looked into her face.

"I guess you're not the only one that enjoys a little porn," he said with an awkward smile as he realized the loose-fitting pants were not hiding his erection.

Ms. Cindy looked back down at the bulge in his pants and then she looked into his eyes. "Is that all you down there?" she asked curiously, she gave a subtle nod down toward his midsection.

Kevin saw the lust in her eyes when she asked him that question. He couldn't believe Ms. Cindy was making a pass at him. It felt a little awkward, but he was turned on by it.

"Is that all you right there?" he asked flirtatiously as he gave a subtle nod down towards her noticeable camel toe.

One thing led to another, and Kevin found himself having sex with Ms. Cindy on her living room sofa. Her performance blew his mind. Her background as a dancer influenced the way she moved during sex. With her long slender legs, she was graceful and poised and he was amazed at how limber and flexible she was as he bent and twisted her every way he could imagine.

****

Chapter 16

"You're gonna have to figure it out, because shame is not strong enough of a feeling to fight fornication and lust. You're not gonna be able to stop doing what you are doing until you truly feel God's conviction in your heart."

-Ms. Cindy

Kevin sat confidently behind the pulpit on his hand-carved, cherry oak Pastor's throne and listened as the choir sung hymns to the packed pews.

Since Kevin's arrival, the church's attendance had increased by more than forty percent. He calmly tapped his feet and hands to the music as he scanned the many faces in the crowd. He smiled at his wife and kids sitting in the front row. He sneakily cut his eyes at Carmen Jones. She winked and smiled as she caught him looking at her. He noticed April staring at him like a lovesick teenage girl. He cracked a smile and gave her a subtle nod, causing her to blush. He looked toward the back of the church and noticed Linda Green standing at Ms. Cindy's post. He scanned the crowd again but didn't see Ms. Cindy. He had been really looking forward to seeing her after her amazing performance a few days ago.

**

After the morning service had ended, Kevin summoned Linda Green to his office.

"Where is Ms. Cindy?" he asked.

"I don't know. She called me this morning and asked if I could fill in for her."

"Is she sick or something?"

"I don't know, I didn't ask no questions," she replied.

Kevin knew she was lying when she said she didn't ask any questions. *She didn't earn the nickname old nosey Linda by not asking questions,* he thought as he stared back in her face, but he wasn't put off by her elusiveness. As soon as she left his office, he immediately tried to call Ms. Cindy. Her phone went straight to voicemail. He tried two more times and still no answer, so he decided to drive over to her house to check in on her.

**

When Kevin arrived at Ms. Cindy's house, she answered the door wearing a shiny silk pink pajama set. She didn't greet him. She just opened the door, turned, and walked to her living room.

"Are you alright?" he asked as he closed the door behind him and followed her into her living room.

"I'm okay," she replied.

"We missed you at service today," he said awkwardly as he tried to read her mood.

"And I missed being there too," she said in a dreary tone.

"So why weren't you there?"

"Because I have to pack."

"Pack for what?"

"Because I'm leaving town."

"What do you mean you're leaving town?"

"I'm going to live with my daughter in Arizona."

"Why? Is it because of what happened between us?"

"Yes, it is." She nodded her head calmly, and then she looked into his eyes. "I can't set a foot back in that church after what we did."

"Ms. Cindy, please, let's talk about this," Kevin pleaded.

"Pastor Tyler, I'm not going to smile in your wife's face after what we did," she said, raising her voice at him. "I'm too old to play those kinds of games," she stated firmly. "I'm a grown woman, and I knew what I was doing with you was wrong. I can own up to my mess, but I'm not going to hang around here to be one of your wenches."

"One of my wenches? What are you talking about?"

"Pastor, please. There ain't no secrets in a black church," she scoffed at him. "Ushers hear and see everything that goes on in the church. I see the way Deacon Jones's wife looks at you during service and old nosey Linda Green lives right down the street from Sistah April. She told me that she sees your car parked around the corner, two or three times a week."

Her words surprised him. He couldn't believe she knew about him. He thought his sinful acts were hidden from everyone's eyes.

"Who else knows?" he asked nervously.

"I don't know. I think just me and Nosey Linda, but Dyersburg is a small town. It's going to eventually get out."

"Why didn't you say something about this to me before today?" he asked timidly.

"Because it ain't none of my business. My job is to serve God and the church. It ain't my place to discuss the Pastor's business," Ms. Cindy stressed with caution. "David told King Saul in 1 Samuel 26:23, *I will stretch not my hand against the Lord's anointed.* God anointed you to be a Pastor. It's up to Him, not me, as to when or if your mess comes to light."

Kevin lowered his head and burst into tears. Ms. Cindy lowered her head to look into his eyes. She put her finger under his chin and gently raised his head back up. "Are you crying out of shame, because your secrets are exposed, or are you crying because you feel God's conviction in your heart?" she asked as she tenderly wiped his tears with her fingers.

"I don't know." He shrugged his shoulders.

"You're gonna have to figure it out, because shame is not a strong enough feeling to fight fornication and lust. You're not gonna be able to stop doing what you're doing until you truly feel God's conviction in your heart," she explained, and then she leaned over and kissed his forehead. She grabbed his hand and led him to the door. "I'm going to be leaving in a couple of days, so this is goodbye. I wish you well, Pastor Tyler."

****

Chapter 17

Beware of false prophets, which come to you in sheep's clothing, but inwardly they are ravening wolves.

-Mathew 7:15

Kevin had been numb for days thinking about how he ruined Ms. Cindy's life and ran her out of town. The guilt had been tormenting him, and slowly eating away at his soul. He had to confess his sins and get the guilty weight of his adulterous affairs off his chest. He needed someone he could trust and confide in. He picked up his phone several times to call Reverend Stokes, but he quickly hung up before it even started ringing. He was too ashamed to admit his transgressions to his beloved mentor, so he decided to call Reverend Carver.

Reverend Joe Carver was the pastor of the largest black congregation in Dyersburg. His church was located on the west side of town, in the heart of one of the city's poorest black neighborhoods. He was also the president of Dyersburg's Black Pastors Association. Kevin met him at his meet and greet dinner when he first moved to town from Atlanta.

Reverend Carver had been pastoring for more than forty years. He was a seasoned, seventy-one-year-old pastor and reminded Kevin of Reverend Stokes. They often met for lunch since Kevin's arrival and the two had formed a close relationship, similar to the relationship he had with Reverend Stokes. He and Kevin had been guest preachers at each other's churches, and Kevin trusted him. He invited Reverend Carver to lunch with hopes he could give him guidance like Reverend Stokes usually did.

They agreed to meet at *Ms. Annie Mae's Soul Food Kitchen.* When Kevin pulled up to the restaurant, he noticed Reverend Carver's white Mercedes was already in the parking lot. He looked at his watch.

"He's a little early," Kevin said to himself. He smiled as he thought about Reverend Stokes and how he used to show up early to their lunch engagements.

When Kevin entered, he saw Reverend Carver sitting at a table in the corner near the large tinted window that faced the parking lot. The reverend's eyes gleamed as he watched Kevin walk toward him. He stood and they shook hands. Kevin took a step back to admire Reverend Carver's outfit.

"Look at you, old man." Kevin chuckled. "You got on the Gucci button-down with the matching Gucci slacks, *and* you're even wearing the Gucci loafers."

Besides being pastors, the two men had fashion in common. They both loved to wear expensive designer clothes.

"I might be old, but I'm still in style," Reverend Carver joked as he sat back down in his chair.

Reverend Carver could easily pass for a man in his mid-fifties. He looked good for his age. He stood a little over six feet tall, with a slim build and a full head of low-cut, wavy gray hair.

Reverend Carver ordered the fried chicken with mashed potatoes and gravy and Kevin ate his usual of fried catfish with baked beans and coleslaw. They enjoyed their meal while discussing Trump politics and the NBA playoffs.

After finishing his lunch, Reverend Carver leaned over to Kevin. "Now, Pastor Tyler, tell me what's really on your mind."

"What are you talking about?" Kevin asked.

"When you called me this morning, you said you had something serious to discuss with me. I know Donald Trump and LeBron James ain't the serious issue you had on your mind."

Kevin took a deep breath and sighed, and in a split second, his mood went from relaxed to tense. While eating lunch, he had changed his mind and decided not to say anything about his illicit affairs, but now that Reverend Carver had asked, Kevin decided to confess.

"I need your advice on something," Kevin said with a nervous expression on his face.

"Okay," Reverend Carver nodded. The look on Kevin's face put him on alert that this was something serious. He adjusted his chair and leaned forward, "What's on your mind son?"

"I...I have uhh..." Kevin suddenly stopped. He turned his head and blinked a few times to prevent any tears from escaping his eyes. He turned back to Reverend Carver and quickly pushed the words out. "I've been having an affair with a member of my church."

Reverend Carver leaned back in his chair and paused for a minute before responding. "Does your wife know?"

"No, sir!"

"Has it gotten out among your congregation?"

"I don't think so."

"So, what's the problem?" Reverend Carver smirked.

"What's the problem?" Kevin repeated in a slightly louder voice. He was surprised by Reverend Carver's nonchalant response. "The problem is that I cheated on my wife. I committed adultery," Kevin said in a loud, animated whisper, and then he looked around the restaurant and over his shoulder as if he were paranoid that someone was listening.

"Welcome to the club," he said to Kevin.

"What club?" Kevin asked. "Are you saying that you've dealt with this issue?"

"Of course! What Pastor hasn't?" Reverend Carver said calmly.

"How did you deal with it? How did you get through it?" Kevin asked eagerly. He felt relieved. He was in the presence of a fellow pastor that could understand what he was going through. Now he felt confident that Reverend Carver could guide him through his dilemma.

"It's not how *did* I deal with it, it's how *do* I manage it," Reverend Carver shot his response back at him.

"What do you mean?"

"Look at me, son. I'm seventy-one years old. I'm an old man, and I can't afford to turn down none of that good, clean, young pussy sittin' around in my church."

Kevin frowned. He was taken aback by what he heard come out of the Reverend's mouth, and his face visibly showed his displeasure in the Reverend's last statement.

"How can you say something like that and still consider yourself a man of God?" Kevin huffed.

"Let me tell you a true story, Brother Pastor," Reverend Carver said. "My grandfather was a Pastor. His name was Reverend Franklin J. Carver. He was a tall man with wide shoulders and a deep voice, and he could preach the roof off a church." Reverend Carver smiled and gazed out of the window as his mind had transported him back in time and he could hear his grandfather preaching.

"But back then, preaching didn't pay the bills. Therefore, my grandfather and his brother, which was my great-uncle, owned a butcher shop. It was a little red building right off Forest Street, over on the west side of town, not far from my church. Everyone called it the Meat Market. They did pretty well too, but they weren't the only butcher shop in town. So, to make a little extra money, once or twice a week, my grandfather would pack up his meat truck and he would go sell and deliver meat to the black communities in the smaller surrounding counties.

One summer, when I was eight years old, he took me with him to deliver his meat. We drove through Lake, Obion, and Lauderdale Counties in one day. That was the most traveling I had ever done in my young life. I was a young country boy and green to the business, but I noticed something odd. My grandfather would charge different prices to different people. It wasn't by county or city, some people he would just charge fifteen-cent per pound, another twenty-cent per pound and some he would even go as high as twenty-five-cent. I could not understand his method, so I asked my grandfather why he charged each person at different prices. And he said to me, 'Because not everybody is the same.' So I asked him, 'How do you know who to charge more and who to charge less?' And he looked at me and said, 'The dumber they look, the more you charge.' I looked at him just like you're looking at me right now, and in my eight-year-old, self-righteous voice, I said, 'Granddaddy, you're a preacher, and that ain't right.' And he said to me, 'Who am I hurting? The one that paid twenty-five-cent a pound is just as happy and grateful as the one that paid fifteen-cent. As long as everybody is happy... where is the harm? If the ones that are paying more don't find out about the ones paying less...no harm is done'

"Stop!" Kevin interrupted him. "I don't need to hear anymore. "So the lesson in that story is that as long as everybody is happy, it's alright to cheat?" Kevin asked in a condescending tone.

Reverend Carver sighed and shook his head out of frustration after realizing Kevin wasn't getting the message he was trying to convey.

"What I'm trying to say is that we are just *men*," Reverend Carver emphasized. "We're just average men that have been called by God to do a job. And our job as pastors is to feed and tend to the flock that God has put in our care. And if a young woman in my congregation is having sexual desires, she's gonna get it whether I give it to her or not. And trust me when I say this, don't no young woman want to read the Bible and pray when she's home alone and all hot and wet between her legs. I've tried it and it don't work. So, it's better for her if I come over and fulfill her needs rather than some young thug that's guaranteed to lead her away from the Lord."

"Average men!" Kevin repeated in disagreement. "We are so much more than average. We are *men of God!*" he said through clenched teeth.

"And what does that mean?" Reverend Carver quickly snapped the question at Kevin.

"It means that we have been entrusted with the Word of God, and that makes us more than just average men." Kevin raised his voice and pounded his fist on the table.

"Calm down, Brother Pastor," Reverend Carver whispered as he looked around the restaurant at the nosey eyes watching their heated discussion. "That type of thinking is why there is so much pressure on preachers and pastors in today's time."

"Explain," Kevin said as he leaned back in his seat with his arms folded across his chest.

"We're not living back in the Old Testament days of Moses and Elijah when God would pick one man to deliver His Word. We live in the New Testament era of the Holy Spirit. God's Will and Words are flowing freely through every born-again believer. They just have to open their eyes and realize it." Reverend Carver said before pausing to wet his mouth with a sip of iced tea.

"That uneducated, Holy Ghost-filled, young man sitting in the back of my church is just as much a man of God as either one of us. But our titles as pastors put us on a higher pedestal. There are women in my congregation that will cuss and act a fool in front of their husbands, but not in front of me. Do you know what that means?"

Kevin shook his head. "No."

"That means she respects me more and holds me in higher esteem than she does the man she's married to, and that ain't right. That's backward. Ephesians 5:33 says a wife is supposed to reverence her husband, and Peter 3:5 says, wives should be in subjection to their *own* husbands. Anytime a woman looks at another man with wider eyes than she does her husband, that's a recipe for disaster. Why would a man mistreat his wife, and then send her to me every Sunday? What am I supposed to do with that? You have just put a sorry, no-good man of the house up against a powerful man of God. The man of the house can't weigh up. How could he? It's easy for me to present myself as the perfect man of God for an hour and a half every Sunday."

There was a momentary silence as Reverend Carver waited for Kevin's response, but Kevin wasn't feeling the Reverend's logic, so he remained quiet.

"My congregation is eighty-five percent female," Reverend Carver said. "Do you know how I keep them in line?"

Kevin shook his head as he took a sip of tea.

"With my shepherd's rod...I keep them in line with my shepherd's rod," Reverend Carver stated.

Kevin spit his tea out as he burst out laughing. Those words sounded funny coming out of Reverend Carver's seventy-one-year-old mouth, but what made Kevin laugh even harder was that Reverend Carver was dead serious.

"You're laughing, but I'm serious," Reverend Carver said. "Psalms 23:4 *...thy rod and thy staff they comfort* *me.* I teach them biblical lessons and I comfort them with my shepherd's rod."

"You have the largest black congregation in the city. How can an old man like you handle all of those women?" Kevin asked jokingly.

Reverend Carver cut his eyes at Kevin and in a sly tone he said, "I can do in thirty minutes what it takes these young men two hours to do. Trust me, this old man knows how to please a woman."

Kevin couldn't help but laugh. Reverend Carver was coming off comical.

"Is the young woman you're having the affair with married?" he asked Kevin.

"One of them is married."

"What do you mean one of them? I thought it was only one woman."

"No...actually it's three."

"Three! And you're sitting there trying to judge me," he scoffed at Kevin.

"I'm not trying to judge you. I just thought you could help me."

"I'm going to be honest with you, Brother Pastor. I don't think I'm the right person to help you with this problem. Besides, why would you want to stop? You've got free rein to have sex with as many women as you can handle."

"I want to stop because I love my wife, and I know that it's wrong.

"If you feel that passionately about it, just stop doing it," Reverend Carver suggested.

"It ain't that easy," Kevin said hopelessly. "The sex just feels too good, and these women are doing things to me that my wife won't do."

"I fool around because I want to, but if I wanted to stop, I could stop, because I can get all the good freaky sex I want from my wife," Reverend Carver bragged. "I'm twenty-two years older than my First Lady." He smiled.

"I can't say that about my wife. Rená was a virgin when I married her, and her sex game hasn't evolved at all over the years."

"A VIRGIN?"

"Yes, sir."

"Were you a virgin too?"

"No, sir. I had been out there in the streets sexing women for years before I married Rená."

"That's your problem," Reverend Carver slapped the table and smiled as if he had just had a eureka moment.

"What do you mean?"

"I made the same mistake the first time I got married."

"What mistake are you talking about?" Kevin asked.

"I married a virgin too," Reverend Carver said and then he lowered his head and shook it pitifully from side to side. "And it was one of the worst mistakes of my life."

"Why?"

"Because it's alright to marry a virgin if both of you are virgins, or if the man is inexperienced too. But if the man has a lot of sexual experience and he's used to freaky women doing freaky things to him, then that virgin novelty wears off real fast. His body starts to crave those strange things those street girls used to do."

"You're right." Kevin smiled.

"After I divorced my first wife, I went out and found myself an ex-ho turned church girl," Reverend Carver stated.

"A WHAT?"

"An ex-ho turned church girl," Reverend Carver repeated.

"What is that?" Kevin laughed.

"You've met my sweet little wife."

Kevin nodded. "Yes."

"Between you and me, before she found God, she was one of the biggest hoes in Ripley, Tennessee. But now, she's the perfect little preacher's wife. I think all Pastors should marry an ex-ho turned church girl."

"Why do you say that?"

"First of all, an ex-ho has some history, she's been through some stuff, which gives her the ability to relate to you and your many shortcomings. Secondly, she knows the power of God's forgiveness and the goodness of His mercy. She won't judge you, because she knows what God has brought her through, and third and most important, she knows how to please her man in bed. You get the benefits of all the skills and tricks she learned while she was outside in the streets." Reverend Carver stopped to take a sip of tea.

"And let me tell you something else, ain't nothing more worthless than a beautiful woman that don't know how to please her man in bed...she's like a big dry steak with no flavor—just a dead piece of meat."

Kevin left the lunch meeting with more questions than answers. Reverend Carver was not the man he thought he was. He realized Reverend Carver was just another southern cliché...a slick, fried chicken-eating, womanizing, pulpit pimp. *He's no Reverend Stokes,* Kevin thought as he drove away from the restaurant.

****

Chapter 18

"Beware of the spirit of Potiphar's Wife…"

-The Pastor's Book of Warnings

Tears streamed down Pam's cheeks as she sat on the leather couch in the Pastor's office, pouring her soul out to First Lady Rená Tyler. Rená sat next to her with a box of tissue in one hand, while gently patting and rubbing Pam's back with the other hand.

"God will not put more on you than you can bear," Rená said softly.

Kevin sat behind his desk on the other side of the room and listened to Pam complain and bawl her eyes out about her no-good, abusive husband. She initially requested a counseling session with him, but he explained to her that he would only counsel a female member with his wife present. Pam was considering divorcing her husband and she needed their guidance.

"But the Bible says divorce is forbidden," Pam whimpered to Rená.

"Forbidden for everything except fornication," Rená replied.

Kevin walked from behind his desk and sat on the couch next to his wife. He leaned across Rená's lap and

99

spoke firmly to Pam. "God didn't intend for anyone to stay in an abusive marriage either."

During her eleven years of marriage to Parnell Snipes, Pam had been cheated on and beaten more times than she could remember, but she never forgot the first time he hit her. One day at work, an old high school boyfriend smiled at her in front of Parnell. Later that day, after they made it home, he accused her of sleeping with him and he beat her all through the night while she was pregnant with their first child.

Despite having two more kids, their marriage had never recovered. From Pam's point-of-view, their relationship had grown increasingly worse over the years. She had caught him cheating so many times, that it no longer bothered her. Some nights, she was glad when he didn't come home. Her house was peaceful when he wasn't around.

Pam was not always so accepting of his cheating. There was a time when she would fuss and raise hell whenever she'd hear about him and another woman. But a few years ago, she had her sister follow him from work, and she caught him red-handed at a hotel with one of her coworkers. Pam figured that since she caught him naked in a hotel room with another woman that this would be her turn to act a fool and go off on him. Instead, she ended up getting the worst beating of her life. Parnell twisted things around and accused her of not trusting him. He said she was the one in the wrong for having her sister follow him from work. After that ordeal, Pam quit fussing or even caring about his infidelities. Parnell even tried beating her for not caring anymore. He'd say that if she didn't care about what he was doing, then *she* must be cheating.

Pam had been sexually frustrated in her marriage for years. Their sex life had gotten so bad that she preferred not to have sex at all. They both worked eight-hour shifts at the same factory. But when they got home, Parnell would either nap or meet up with friends, while she made sure the kids got home safe and maintained the house. By bedtime, she would be exhausted which was also the time Parnell wanted to have sex. Sometimes, she'd try to explain how tiring her day was, but that would always result in a fight. She found herself often giving in just to avoid conflict. And she'd often compare her sex life to that of Whoopi Goldberg's character from *The Color Purple*. He would just get on top, do his business and roll over. She couldn't remember the last time he'd even kissed or caressed her breasts, and it had been so long since she had an orgasm that she wondered if they even existed anymore.

Over the years, Parnell's verbal abuse outweighed the physical. He would always put her down. He'd tell her, *"Ain't no other man gonna want you with three kids."* He called her stupid bitch more than he called her by name. He constantly complained about her weight gain but would pick fights whenever she tried to diet and lose weight. He'd claim she was trying to look good for other men.

Finally, adding insult to injury, Parnell had a gambling problem. Every other Friday, after getting paid, he drove straight to the casinos in Mississippi. He rarely ever won, most of the time, he would break even. Occasionally he'd lose his entire check, which was when he'd come home and pick a fight with Pam for "jinxing" him with bad luck.

Kevin listened with amazement as Pam shared her problems. He couldn't understand how a man could treat his wife so badly. What baffled Kevin, even more, was the fact that she was still married to such an unstable man.

He thought about what Reverend Carver said to him a few days ago. *"How can a man mistreat his wife and then send her to me?"* Suddenly he had an idea. It was as if a light bulb popped on in his head. *I should try Reverend Carver's shepherd's rod method on Sistah Pam,* he thought as he continued to listen to her problems.

****

Chapter 19

"Thank you, Pastor Tyler. I needed that."

-Pamela Snipes

A week had passed since Pam's counseling session, and Kevin and Rená had kept a close eye on her. They recommended that she call the police and leave the next time her husband tried to beat on her.

Kevin was on his way to her house to check on her, at least that was the excuse he would use when he showed up at her doorstep unannounced. He knew, from listening during her counseling sessions, that her husband would be gambling in Mississippi. He also knew, from overhearing his wife talk to her on the phone, that her kids had gone bowling with her sister and wouldn't be returning home until later in the evening.

Kevin parked in front of her house and knocked on the door with the sole purpose of comforting her with his 'shepherd's rod'.

"Hey, Pastor Tyler. How are you doing?"Pam answered the door with a smile, wearing a pair of frumpy looking cotton grey sweatpants, a faded blue t-shirt, white crocs, and a pink bonnet. "What brings you by?"

"I was driving through the neighborhood, and I decided to stop by and check on you and the kids."

"Come in," she said, stepping to the side allowing him to enter her home. "The kids aren't here. They went bowling with my sister."

"How have you been?" he asked as he took a seat on her living room couch.

"It's been about the same. Parnell hasn't tried to fight me this week," she said as she sat down on the loveseat across from him. "I'm just glad it's the weekend and he's gone to Mississippi."

Kevin was nervous, but he had made his mind up He's definitely going to comfort her with his shepherd's rod. He just had to wait for the right moment to make his move. "Whatever you're cooking sure smells good," he said, sniffing the air.

"Ooh, I almost forgot." She jumped up and rushed into the kitchen.

He watched closely as she moved around in her sweatpants and t-shirt. He could tell by the way her huge breast flopped around in her loose-fitted t-shirt she wasn't wearing a bra, and even though she was a little on the chunky side, her butt looked like two basketballs bouncing around in the back of her pants. Kevin remained seated for a minute before building up enough courage to slide into the kitchen.

"Is everything alright in here?" he asked as he gradually made his way inside.

"Yes, sir. I just had to take my pot roast out of the oven. I almost forgot about it," she said. She turned her back to him to cut into her roast, making sure it had cooked all the way through.

"It smells delicious," he commented as he deliberately eased close behind her, pressing his chest to her back and his shepherd's rod to her backside.

She felt his presence close behind her and she jumped in a nervous uncomfortable way. "Pastor, what are you doing?" her voice quivered as she froze and shifted her eyes, too afraid to turn around.

"Shh... just take a deep breath and relax," he whispered in her ear as he pressed his erection even harder against her butt, and then he reached around under her shirt, cuffed her bare breast in each hand and began fondling and caressing her large, neglected melons.

Pam's entire body trembled as she felt his warm breath on the back of her neck. She was afraid but aroused at the same time. "Pastor, we can't be doing this," she panted heavily, but she didn't stop him. Instead, she wrapped her hands around his hands and squeezed them tighter around her breast.

Kevin heard her words, but he also felt her lust as she moaned and pushed her butt back against his erection. He smiled, and then licked his lips and planted a sloppy wet kiss on the back of her neck.

"Ooooh," Pam moaned loudly as his warm wet kiss sent a tingling sensation through her body.

I've got her. He remembered hearing her tell Rená that her husband doesn't kiss her anymore, so he greedily began kissing all over the back of her neck and down her shoulders. He turned her around, lifted her shirt, and gave her huge breasts more attention than her husband had in the last ten years.

Pam was thoroughly enjoying everything her pastor was doing to her and she decided she was not going to let this opportunity get away from her, and without any inhibitions, she shoved her jogging pants down her apple bottom, shimmying out of them till they reached her ankles and left them on the kitchen floor. She grabbed his hand, locked the front door, and led him to her bedroom.

Kevin felt like superman after comforting Pam with his shepherd's rod. *Reverend Carver was right. She needed me, and it can't be too wrong if it helped her.* He reasoned to himself as he thought about how he made her body shake and convulse four times in less than thirty minutes. She cried real tears after each orgasm.

"Thank you, Pastor Tyler. I needed that," Pam said with tears still in her eyes.

"That's what I'm here for. Just remember to keep this between you and me."

"I promise I won't tell a soul."

"I know you won't," he said as he leaned over and kissed her. "If you ever need me again, just let me know."

"I will." She nodded as she watched him walk out of her bedroom. "Parnell would beat the hell out of me if he found out about this..." she said to herself while staring at the wet spots on her bedsheets. "But I'm gonna do this again." She smiled. "That was worth an ass-whoopin'." A giggle escaped from her lips as she pulled the sex-stained sheets off her bed.

****

Chapter 20

"You're not the first whorish preacher I've met. To be honest with you, I haven't met many preachers that weren't."

-Sister Linda Green

"Good afternoon, Pastor Tyler." Linda Green stood in the doorway of the Pastor's office and greeted Kevin as he sat behind his desk. She had permanently taken over the head usher's position since Ms. Cindy's departure, and one of her many responsibilities was to supervise the weekly cleaning of the church. Once a week, she and about eight volunteers met up at the church to vacuum the carpet, dust the pews, and clean the lavatories. And she made herself personally responsible for cleaning the Pastor's office.

"Good afternoon to you too, Sistah Green." Kevin smiled. "Come in. What can I do for you?"

"I'm just here to clean your office."

"Oh, okay," he said as he noticed the vacuum and the cleaning cart behind her. "I'll get out of your way in just a second," he said as he stood.

"You won't be in my way. If you can stand the sound of the vacuum cleaner, you can stay right there."

"Nah, I'm going to get up out of here," Kevin said, while stuffing his paperwork into his briefcase. "But I do need to have a word with you before I go."

"Okay," she replied.

Kevin remembered what Ms. Cindy told him the last time he talked with her, *Old nosey Sistah Green lives down the street from April. She told me she sees your car parked around the corner two or three times a week.* He had been wanting to question her about it for some time, but he never found the right moment. Now would be the perfect time to confront her, but he had to be careful. She was a big strong country girl with a reputation for being quick-tempered and he heard she liked to fight.

"Before Ms. Cindy left town, she told me you said that you thought I was messing around with Sistah April."

"I didn't tell her I *thought* you were messing around with April; I told her I *knew* you were messing around with April," she said with a frown.

"Well, it ain't true. So stop spreading that lie," Kevin growled at her.

"Listen here, Pastor Tyler. I'm a grown woman," she snapped. She pursed her lips and narrowed her eyes at him. "I ain't gon' lie *to* you, and I ain't gon' lie *on* you. I told Ms. Cindy exactly what was told to me."

"Whoever told you that lied on me and Sistah April. So stop spreading that lie," he said with a raised voice.

"She ain't gonna lie on herself," she shot back at him.

"Who is she?" Kevin huffed.

"APRIL!" she shouted.

"Sistah April?"

"YES," Linda said as she stood defiantly in front of him with her hands on her hips. "April told me herself that y'all were messing around."

"What? That doesn't even make sense. What did she do, just walk up to you and tell you we were having an affair?"

"Nope, I asked her," she retorted. "They call me nosey for a reason. If I see something, I'm gon' ask questions. I asked her what was you doin' going over her house two and three times a week. And she didn't hesitate to tell all of her business. She told me y'all were having sex, *and* she said it was good. She even said you was packin' and you be goin' down on her."

Kevin looked confused as she spilled her guts to him. He couldn't believe April was being loose-lipped with their business. He was also wondering why Linda hadn't exposed their affair to the rest of the congregation. *She must want a sample of what April is getting.* He checked out her tiny breasts and wide hips. *She's got a big booty for a woman in her late fifties.*

"How are things between you and Brother Green?" Kevin asked just to test the waters.

"FINE!" she exclaimed with her nostrils flared open. She knew where he was trying to go with that question. "I never have, and I never will cheat on my husband," she said, then she stared him down with her jaws clenched tight.

"You don't have to get defensive. I just asked about your husband. I didn't say anything about you cheating on him."

"Mmm humph," she scoffed as she frowned and looked him up and down.

There was an eerie silence between them for a few minutes. She suspiciously cut her eyes at him as she began unwrapping the cord to the vacuum cleaner.

"I need to ask you one more thing before I go."

"What else do you gotta ask me?"

"Can you tell me why you haven't exposed April and me to the rest of the congregation?"

"Because *I will not stretch forth my hand against the Lord's anointed.*" Just like Ms. Cindy, she superstitiously quoted 1 Samuel 26:23. "Whateva mess you got going on in your life is between you and God. God anointed you to be our Pastor, so it's up to Him to expose you in His own time."

"It doesn't bother you to know that you're sitting under a pastor that's having an affair with one of his members?"

"Nope, why should it? I ain't married to you."

"But I'm preaching you a Word that I'm not living up to myself," Kevin said anxiously, he wanted to know why she didn't have a problem with him sleeping with April.

"You're not the first whorish preacher I've met. To be honest with you, I haven't met many preachers that weren't," she said as she noticed the inner conflict going on inside of him. She paused for a moment to allow her mood to project a sense of peace toward him, and then she softened her voice. "Do you know that story in the Old Testament about that talking donkey?"

"I'm a pastor, of course I know that story. You're referring to the story about Balaam in Numbers 22:28."

"Yeah, that's it." She smiled. "My momma used to say it like this. If God can send his Word through a donkey, then He can send it through a whorish preacher. She used to say that if a frog comes preaching the truth, you better sit there and listen to him."

"Okay," Kevin replied somberly as he walked out of his office. His head was spinning in a daze. He couldn't wrap his mind around what she just said. He knew she was trying to encourage him, but he felt insulted. She called him a whorish preacher and then she compared him to a donkey and a frog.

Kevin drove around town chewing over the conversation he had with Linda Green. He stopped by April's house to set her straight about telling their business, but by the time he made it over there, her son was asleep in bed. They had sex and he never mentioned it.

****

Chapter 21

"Beware of the Jezebel spirit that lurks throughout the church..."

-The Pastor's Book of Warnings

"I'll do it." Beverly Lawson eagerly raised her hand and volunteered to make signs for New Hope's annual spring yard sale.

"Thank you, Sistah Beverly. Would anyone like to help her with this task?" Kevin asked the small crowd of about forty members scattered out among the pews. "Don't everybody raise their hands at the same time," he commented jokingly, trying to lighten the mood at the always-gloomy monthly church meeting.

However, no one volunteered to help Beverly. Some of the women even hissed and turned their nose up at her, but Beverly didn't care, she just lifted her chin high and straightened her shoulders as she sat on the pew by herself. She was used to church women treating her like a disease. They had never greeted her with the customary smile or hug. They only give her funny looks and nasty whispers. Occasionally, one of them would walk up to her and make a snide remark about how tight her dress fit or how much of her cleavage was showing.

Kevin looked around with disgust at the way the other women were treating her. "Just do the best you can, and if you need any help, you can call on me or my wife for assistance," he said to her.

"Thank you," she mouthed back silently to him, then she smiled and batted her long designer eyelashes at him.

Beverly was a thirty-five-year-old single mother with a teenage daughter. She had the disgraceful reputation of being a home-wrecker and whore. She moved from church to church, seducing, and beguiling older, more financially stable, married men. But she wasn't exclusive to just church-going men, any man with money was a potential target for her. She didn't care if he was married or single, saint or sinner, if he had what she wanted, she was going to get him.

New Hope Pentecostal Church was the fifth church she had joined in the past eight years. Gossip and malicious rumors had run her away from every other church she'd belonged to in the past. She decided to join New Hope when she heard about their wealthy new pastor from Atlanta. She assumed that since he's new to the town, he didn't know about her ruthless reputation. She planned to get in and quickly seduce him before anyone could warn him about her.

Beverly was highly skilled in the art of seduction. And despite being unemployed, she lived in a luxury apartment, drove a brand-new Escalade, and always rocked the latest designer clothes. Her apartment was filled with expensive name-brand furniture. Not to mention the fact that she always kept her and her daughter's nails done, and hair laid tight.

She learned everything she knew from her mother and she was determined to teach her daughter the same lessons. When Beverly was just thirteen, she realized her body had changed. Her breasts were full and perky, her hips had spread wide, and her butt became round and plump. She began to walk and dress like her mom. One day, she noticed her mother's boyfriend looking at her with lust-filled eyes and then he propositioned her. He told young Beverly that he would give her twenty-five dollars if she would sit on his lap for five minutes. Terrified, she ran and told her mother. But her mother didn't give her the response she had expected. Instead, she scolded young Beverly and told her never to turn down easy money from a weak-minded man. And then she schooled her daughter.

"Didn't you ask me for twenty dollars yesterday so you could by a damn Mariah Carey CD?"

"Yes, Ma'am," thirteen-year-old *Beverly said while nodding with tears in her eyes.*

"And what did I tell you?"

"You said you ain't got no twenty dollars to be spending on no CD."

"Do you still want that CD?" She tested her daughter. If Beverly answered no, she would have respected it and revealed that she had put her boyfriend up to propositioning her, but if she answered yes, she'd allow her to sit in his lap. "Well, I'm waiting for an answer. Do you still want the CD or not?"

Beverly nodded, knowing exactly what her mother would make her do.

"Well then," her mother said as she looked at her as if she was a grown woman. "You better go in there and use what you got to get what you want."

Beverly calmly walked into the living room and sat on his lap, and ever since that day, she used her body and good looks to get everything she wanted out of life.

Volunteering to help with the church's yard sale was her way of getting close to the Pastor. She figured that all she had to do was get him alone. No man had ever been able to resist her charm. Beverly had mastered her techniques. Once she grabbed her mark's attention, she would pretend to be lonely and misunderstood. She'd seduce him with her beauty and reel him in by feeding his need to save her.

Kevin would prove to be a much easier mark than she had expected. She had no idea that his conscience had already been sullied with the feelings of guilt and unrighteousness. He no longer had the moral constitution of a married preacher. Passion and lust controlled his desires.

Kevin's eyes secretly roamed Beverly's body during the entire meeting as she sat by herself on the front row. Linda and Jackie warned him about her the first day she stepped into the church. But he couldn't help but think to himself. *How can such a beautiful and innocent looking woman have such a terrible reputation.* The thought of her being such a nasty slut turned him on and had him curious about the extent of her sexual skills. He wanted to experience whatever she had to offer.

After the meeting, Kevin asked Beverly to stay back so he could have a brief word with her in his office. He wanted to talk a little more in detail about the signs she volunteered to make, at least that was what he told her.

"Have a seat," he said calmly as they walked into his office. He opened the mini-refrigerator. "Would you like some apple juice or Coke?"

"No thank you," she replied, and she intentionally remained standing. Beverly learned at an early age that it's easier to seduce a man while she moved around on her feet. A woman like her, with nice curves, could better show off her assets if she were standing, which also made it easier for her to follow a man's eyes as he admired what was right in front of him.

And Kevin did not disappoint. She instantly recognized the look of lust in his eyes as he inspected her body. He looked at her like a hungry dog stared at a piece of meat, and even though his mouth was talking about the yard sale, his eyes were begging for sex.

Like dangling a delectable morsel of food before a starving man, Beverly paced back and forth as they talked in his office. She had him captivated, and she couldn't allow her mark to get away from her without sealing the deal. She knew from experience that a true seductress must seize the moment.

"Pastor Tyler, have you ever had a three-point-special?" she asked, abruptly changing the subject in the middle of their conversation.

"Uh...I don't know. I've never heard of a three-point-special."

"Now that's hard for me to believe." She smiled at him.

"Does it have anything to do with food or basketball?" he asked.

"No, silly." She laughed and calmly strolled over to him behind his desk and whispered in his ear. "A three-point-special is when a woman allows a man to penetrate all three holes on her body and release his hot fluid in each one of them."

Kevin was instantly aroused, and he suddenly froze when he felt her hand in his lap.

"Meet me at my apartment in an hour, and I'll show you how a three-point-special feels," she said before walking out of his office. She didn't even wait for his response. She could tell by the look on his face and the bulge in his lap that he would accept her offer.

Beverly read him correctly. Kevin couldn't resist the temptation of her three-point-special recommendation. He arrived outside of her apartment in less than forty-five minutes. He sat in his car and watched the clock. About to explode with anticipation, all he could think about was Beverly allowing him to enter every hole on her beautiful body.

Beverly's sixteen-year-old daughter Chanel was leaving the apartment just as he was walking toward the door. She smiled at him. "Hey, Pastor Tyler. Momma is inside waiting for you."

Kevin smiled back at her and kept walking, he couldn't help but think, from the sound of her voice and the look in her eyes that she knew what was about to go down between her mother and him.

Beverly answered the door wearing a short silk robe that barely reached her thighs, which she intentionally left open, allowing him to see that she was naked underneath.

"Hi, Pastor. I was about to call you to tell you not to come over."

"Why, what's wrong?" he asked as he eyeballed her smooth light brown breasts peeking at him through the opening in her robe.

"When I got home from church this evening, my daughter showed me this." She handed him a piece of paper. "It's a final notice from a collection agency. They are going to repossess my Escalade tomorrow if I don't come up with a payment by nine in the morning. I'm sorry but I can't do a three-point-special with all this on my mind. I can't focus, knowing that I'm going to lose my vehicle."

But Kevin was aroused and filled with anticipation. He wanted to experience every inch of her voluptuous body.

"How much is your payment?" he asked.

"$785," she replied bashfully.

"That's all!" Kevin exclaimed with excitement. $785 wasn't enough money to stand in the way of him experiencing his first three-point-special. He reached in his back pocket, pulled out his phone. "Do you have Apple Pay or Zelle?"

Beverly's eyes lit-up. "I have Apple Pay."

He sent her the money and she jumped up and hugged him as if he had just given her a million dollars. "Thank you, Pastor. Thank you so much. I promise you I will pay you back."

"Don't worry about paying it back. I'm just glad I can help."

Beverly didn't say another word. She dropped her robe and led him into her bedroom. She smiled to herself as she closed the bedroom door behind them. The smile was for her daughter. For coming up with the idea of creating a fake final notice letter on her computer about twenty minutes before Kevin arrived. Her Escalade was never in jeopardy of being repossessed. She had it paid off by one of her former suitors less than six months after she drove it off the lot.

****

Chapter 22

"People are not whispering about us like they are about you and April."

- Jackie

Jackie Lawrence stood nervously outside of Pastor Tyler's office. Instead of doing her usual duties as the church's secretary, she had spent the entire morning trying to build up enough courage to confront him about Beverly Lawson. She was at the church meeting a few nights ago and noticed when Beverly stayed back with him after everyone had left.

"Excuse me, Pastor Tyler," she said peeking her head inside of his office. "Can I have a word with you?"

"Sure, come in."

"I know it's not my place to keep saying something to you on this subject, but can you please be careful around Beverly Lawson. I noticed that the two of you stayed back in your office after the meeting the other night."

Kevin leaned back in his chair and smiled at her. He knew Jackie had a crush on him. He still had some of his street sense, and he realized a while ago that she always watched him and warned him about other women. And even though she was in her mid-thirties, he thought it was cute. He was flattered by how overprotective she was of him. "Why are you worried about me and Sistah Beverly? Are you jealous?" He smiled at her.

"No, I'm not jealous." She blushed. "I'm just concerned about you. Beverly is a pro, she's not as naïve and gullible as April."

Kevin quickly sat up straight in his chair. "What does April have to do with this conversation?"

"Everybody can see the way she looks at you."

"The way a woman looks at a man doesn't mean anything. You look at me the same way," he said flirtatiously.

Jackie smiled and turned her head to keep from looking at him. He was joking but she knew there was some truth in his words. She was enamored by everything about him. His lips, his voice, the way he walked, even his smile made her knees weak. It was hard working around him every day. But no matter how infatuated she was with him, she had vowed to herself a long time ago, that she would never fool around with a married man.

"People are not whispering about us like they are about you and April."

"And what are the people saying when they're whispering about me and Sistah April?"

"The rumor is that you two are having an affair."

Kevin sat in silence after Jackie made the statement to him about April. He wondered how many people knew about them, and why hadn't they exposed him.

"Well, is it true?" she blurted out impatiently, as the sharp sound of her voice startled him and interrupted his thoughts.

"Is what true?"

"You and April," she replied with a look on her face that read, *You know what I'm talking about.*

"Yes...It's true." He trusted Jackie and could tell her the truth without hesitation. He knew she had his back.

She stayed silent as she stood in front of him with a blank stare on her face.

"How does that make you feel?" he asked.

"I don't feel anything. That's between you and your wife." Even though she already knew the rumor was true she wished he had lied to her, because now she felt conflicted. A part of her was jealous of April and another part of her was disappointed that the man she thought so highly of was an adulterer.

Kevin could see that she was disturbed by his confession. Her fair complexion made it hard for her to hide her true feelings. Her face turned red when he admitted to his affair, and she shifted nervously when she answered him. As he watched her fidget in front of him, he saw her in a different light. She had always looked like a nerdy secretary in her glasses with her hair pulled back in a bun, and she usually dressed old-fashioned in her pencil skirt and loose-fitting blouse. But today, he could see past her glasses, and her body was what Big Mike used to call skinny-thick. She was tall and slender with just enough weight in all the right places.

"Take your glasses off," he ordered her.

"Why?" she asked timidly.

Kevin stood and walked around his desk. Invading her personal space, he reached his hand out and gently removed her glasses then sat them down on his desk. "I just want to see what you look like without them."

Jackie closed her eyes and lowered her head.

"Open your eyes and let me see you," Kevin said as he carefully put his finger under her chin, lifting it so he could see her eyes. "Why do you hide those beautiful hazel eyes behind those glasses?"

Jackie didn't answer him—she couldn't answer him. She was so nervous looking back into his eyes that she froze. This was the closest she had ever been to him. She could smell the sweetness of his morning apple juice that still lingered on his breath.

Kevin reached behind her head and pulled out the two bobby pins holding her hair in a bun. "Let me see what you look like with your hair down," he said as he stepped back to get a camera view of her. He watched her as she shook her head and raked her fingers through her hair.

"You're gorgeous," he said, and then he eased up to her and put his hands on her waist. He smiled when she jumped. He knew she was nervous, so he gently pulled her close to him and kissed her.

The first touch of his lips nearly took her breath away. Jackie thought she was going to faint. But she quickly returned the kiss as their tongues interlocked.

"Wait—" Jackie said as she pushed away from him and took a step back. "I can't do this. I can't go there with you." It took everything she had to stop. It was the best kiss she'd ever had. She had been waiting her entire life for a kiss like that, but she couldn't go against her vows.

"What's wrong?" he asked her.

"You're married."

"So what."

"That may not mean anything to you, but it does to me, and I just can't do it." She grabbed her glasses off his desk and put them back on.

Jackie's loyalty and friendship were worth more to him than a quickie, so Kevin returned to his seat behind his desk. "Let's just pretend this didn't happen," he said.

"I can do that." She nodded her head. But she knew she couldn't. She could still feel his lips touching her. She was only glad he did not press the issue. She didn't know if she would have been strong enough to resist him if he would have kept trying.

"Can I ask you a question?"

"Sure," Kevin replied.

"Do you love your wife?"

"Yes, of course, I love my wife."

"Well... if you love her... why do you cheat on her?"

Her question caught him off-guard. He was stuck for a minute. He didn't know what to say or how to answer the question. He had never thought about it like that.

"Are you happy in your marriage?"

"Yeah...I think so."

"So, please, tell me, why do men cheat on good women, because I know First Lady is a good wife to you."

"Why are you asking me these hard questions?"

Jackie took a deep breath and started fumbling nervously with her fingers. "Because, when I was in college, my fiancé cheated on me and got another girl pregnant. That was the worst feeling in the world. He hurt me so bad. But the worst part about it was that I couldn't understand why. I was good to him, and I did everything I could to please him, and he still cheated on me with one of those nasty, hood rat girls."

Kevin picked up on the pain and anger in her voice as she told her story. He still didn't know what to say. He was a man, and he didn't know why men cheated. "I don't know, Jackie," he said to her.

"I guess all men are dogs," she said.

"No, we're not. I was faithful to my wife for seventeen years. I didn't start cheating until we moved here."

"So what's different now?"

"I don't know, but don't give up on men. Some of us may go astray. But we'll eventually find our way back home."

After Jackie left his office, Kevin thought about her question for hours. *Why do men cheat on good women?*

****

Chapter 23

"Well, God ain't gonna bless no lie. So come clean and lay it all out to her."

-Reverend Stokes

"Please turn your Bibles to the book of Matthew chapter five, verse thirteen," Kevin instructed his Sunday morning congregation. He stood confidently in front of the packed pews and looked on as they pulled their Bibles out and began skimming through the pages.

"Let us stand for the reading of God's Word," he said in a calm monotone voice and then read the scripture aloud. *'Ye are the salt of the earth: but if the salt have lost his saviour, wherewith shall it be salted? It is thenceforth good for nothing, but to be cast out and trodden under foot of men'*... Amen... You may be seated."

"The title of today's message is *God's Preservers of Righteousness,*" Kevin announced and then paused momentarily to allow a few handclaps and 'Amens' from the crowd. "When I say preservers of righteousness, I'm talking about you and me—us born again, Holy Ghost-filled church folk... WE ARE THE SALT OF THE EARTH." His words thundered through the speakers as he turned on his preaching voice and then he paused again to take a sip from the glass of water positioned on his custom-built acrylic podium. After sipping his water, he carefully placed the glass back down and picked up the white monogram handkerchief that had been neatly folded next to the glass of water.

Kevin calmly popped the handkerchief open and dabbed the excess water from his lips. "Umph," he mumbled under his breath. He could have sworn he just caught a whiff of Beverly's scent from his hand.

He dabbed his lips again with the handkerchief, but this time, he subtly and intentionally sniffed his fingers as he wiped his mouth. *Oh my God.* The fragrance of her vagina infused his hand, and he at once felt a deep sense of guilt and remorse for what he had just done.

A few minutes before he came out to preach, while the choir was still singing, he and Beverly had a quickie in his office. Kevin instantly began replaying the scene over in his head. He remembered bending her over on his desk with her dress pulled up. He recalled finishing inside of her and then rushing to put on his cassock. He grabbed his Bible and eased out of his office through the sanctuary entrance as she snuck out through the office's back entrance. Then it dawned on him. *I forgot to wash my hands.*

In that instant, feelings of fear and panic ran through his entire body. He looked out at his congregation and his mind went blank. He forgot what he was preaching about. The room started spinning and he became disorientated and confused. His hands began to shake, and his breathing became erratic. Kevin was terrified. He felt as if he had desecrated God's pulpit. He had touched God's Holy Bible and defiled it with the filth of his adulterous hands. Feeling dirty and unclean, he thought

God was going to strike him down dead, right there on the spot.

Oh, God, I'm sorry... Please forgive me, he nervously repeated in his head as his body shook uncontrollably. His breathing became even more erratic as tears began streaming from his eyes.

"Alright now, Pastor," a single voice shouted from the crowded pews.

Kevin began crying loud and uncontrollably.

"Glory hallelujah," another voice shouted as some of the members of the congregation stood and started clapping. They were interpreting Kevin's moment of guilty conviction as a move of the Holy Spirit.

Kevin realized what was going on and decided to play along, "Glory hallelujah," he shouted as he tried to fake his way out of the situation. He knew he was too discombobulated to finish his sermon. "GLORY HALLELUJAH," he shouted again, this time as loud as he could, as tears continued to flow down his face.

More members of the congregation stood, and some even began crying and shouting along with him. Finally, the music director bailed him out. He cued the pianist and drummer to play, which encouraged more members to become moved by the spirit. Kevin started clapping and stomping his feet to the music while crying and shouting. The congregation followed his lead, and for the next twenty minutes, the entire church danced and shouted unto the Lord. Kevin never finished his sermon and once the dancing and shouting ended, he prayed and dismissed the service.

**

"I messed up. I messed up," Kevin cried to the FaceTime image of Reverend Stokes on his iPhone. After nearly having a panic attack in the pulpit, he shook a few hands and then immediately locked himself in his office.

"Calm down, son. What's going on?" Reverend Stokes asked.

"I cheated on Rená. I had sex with one of my members. I smelled her scent on me while I was preaching in the pulpit. I feel like God is going to strike me down." Kevin wept and babbled incoherently.

"Slow down, son. Take a deep breath and tell me everything."

Kevin followed Reverend Stokes' suggestion and took a few deep breaths to try to calm himself down. Then he took his time and revealed everything to his spiritual father.

Reverend Stokes was taken aback by the details of Kevin's candid confession. "Kevin, what in the world were you thinking about? Didn't you read the book I gave you? It should have warned you about how to deal with the different types of women in these small-town churches."

"Yes, sir. I read the book, but I skipped past the sections dealing with adultery and fornication. I didn't think I would ever do that to Rená. I didn't think I'd fall victim to another woman."

"*Wherefore let him that thinketh he standeth, take heed lest he fall,*" Reverend Stokes said.

"What did you say?" Kevin asked.

"I quoted 1Corinthians 10:12, *Wherefore let him that thinketh he standeth, take heed lest he fall.* You didn't take heed son, and now you have fallen into a big pile of mess."

Kevin could hear the disappointment in Reverend Stokes' voice. He felt dirty and embarrassed as the Reverend's eyes peered back at him from his screen.

"I know I messed up, but what should I do?" Kevin cried. He needed to hear a word from the Lord, and Reverend Stokes always came through with divine wisdom and advice.

"First, you have to come clean to your wife and confess your infidelities."

"I can't do that. Rená would leave me in a heartbeat."

"Listen to what I'm telling you, son. You must confess everything to your wife," Reverend Stokes stressed to him.

"Everything?" Kevin raised his voice.

"Yes, everything! Do you want God to bless your marriage?"

"Yes, sir."

"Well, God ain't gonna bless no lie. So come clean and lay it all out to her."

"But what if she leaves me?"

"You can't allow fear to keep you from doing the right thing. Besides, I know Rená, she loves God, and she loves you. She will be upset, and it will take some time, but she will forgive you."

"I don't know about that." Kevin shook his head.

"Trust me, son. Talk to Rená, and then call me back after you're done."

****

Chapter 24

"No, I'm not sick, but I think we need to talk."

-Kevin Tyler

After talking to Reverend Stokes, Kevin hid in his office for a few more hours. He took the long way home and drove slowly as he tried to wrap his mind around how to come clean to his wife about his adulterous affairs. Rená was the sweetest woman he'd ever known, and he didn't know how to justify cheating on her with so many different women.

When he finally walked into the house, Rená and the kids were eating. She had prepared a Sunday dinner for him.

Rená's eyes lit up as soon as her husband entered the dining room. She stopped eating and flashed her smile at him, then quickly pushed away from the table and greeted him with a kiss. "Hey, honey, I tried to wait for you, but the kids were hungry."

"It wasn't me, Daddy. Mikey is the one that couldn't wait on you," Joann said.

"It was you, too, Joann." Mikey scowled at his sister.

"Kick your shoes off and go wash your hands. I'll fix your plate," Rená said to Kevin.

"I'm not hungry," Kevin mumbled before dragging up the stairs to his bedroom.

Rená detected a bit of sadness in his voice, she also noticed that he never looked her in the eyes while she was talking to him, as she watched him drop his head and slump his shoulders while walking up the stairs. Her intuition told her that something serious was going on with her husband. But she didn't immediately follow him to their bedroom. She wanted to give him a little time to sort through whatever he was dealing with. She also wanted to make sure the kids were fed and satisfied before she went upstairs. Rená figured that once she went upstairs, she wouldn't be coming back down. She looked forward to spending some much-needed quality time with him. He looked like he could use her womanly touch tonight.

**

"Hey, honey, what's going on?" Rená asked as she sat down on the bed next to Kevin. He was stretched out on top of the bed in his silk Louis Vuitton pajamas. "Are you sick?"

"No, I'm not sick, but I think we need to talk."

"Okay, let's talk," she said. She had listened to his problems before. In her mind, it was her duty as a wife and First Lady to counsel and support her husband in his times of need.

Kevin braced himself and then he began confessing to his wife. But Rená was so devastated and taking it so hard that he only admitted to the affair with Beverly Johnson. He tried to use Beverly's Jezebel reputation as an excuse for his weakness.

132

"Stop talking to me. Just shut up," Rená shouted at him. She couldn't bear to hear anymore. She didn't want to believe the words that were coming out of her husband's mouth. He was taking her to a place she thought she would never go. How could the man she married hurt her like this? She was so upset that she became physically sick. She rushed to the bathroom and threw-up.

Kevin followed her into the bathroom. "Baby I'm sorry. I made a mistake, and I promise you that it will never happen again," he said, trying to apologize. It hurt him to see his wife on her knees and slumped over the toilet, crying and puking her guts out.

Rená couldn't tell if the pain was in her stomach or her heart, all she knew was that she had to get away from him. Still crying, she stormed past Kevin and ordered the kids to get dressed and without saying another word, she jumped in her Escalade with her kids and drove straight to Atlanta.

She couldn't get the images of her husband making love to another woman out of her head. She felt her world was crumbling. As she drove to Atlanta, she vowed never to return to Dyersburg, Tennessee.

Joann and little Mikey didn't know what was going on. They had never seen their parents fight. All they knew was their mother was crying and it was their father's fault.

****

Chapter 25

"That's exactly what I'm saying. If you don't give him what he wants, another woman will."

-Sheila

Rená sat on her mother's living room sofa crying her eyes out while her three sisters tried to comfort her. After Kevin's devastating confession, she didn't know what to do. The only thing that made sense to her was to go to her mother's house in Atlanta.

"I can't believe Kevin did this to you," her baby sister Joyce said.

"You need to move back here to Atlanta with us," her other sister Sue added as she wrapped her arms around Rená's shoulders.

"Your father is putting the kids to bed," her mother, Rosa Lee said as she walked into the living room. "Now tell me what's going on with you and Kevin," she demanded as she took a seat on the sofa, squeezing in between Rená and Joyce.

Through agonizing tears, Rená recanted all the details of Kevin's confession. "I just don't see how he could do this to me after seventeen years of marriage," she cried.

"I can't believe it either. This doesn't sound like something Kevin would do." Rosa Lee shook her head in disbelief.

"I can believe it." Rená's oldest sister, Sheila, interrupted with her voice slightly raised. "And I don't feel sorry for her either. I told her this was going to happen."

"Sheila! What has gotten into you?" Rosa Lee scolded.

"It's her fault that Kevin cheated on her. I'm just surprised it took this long," Sheila said.

"Girl, what are you talking about?" Joyce asked.

"Tell her, Sue," Sheila ordered.

"Uh-uh. Don't put me in this," Sue snapped at Sheila.

"Just say whatever's on your mind," Rená said to Sheila.

"Okay then..." Sheila smacked her lips and rolled her neck with an attitude. "...when you and Kevin first got married, how many times a week did you tell me y'all were having sex?"

"Twice," Rená answered. There was an awkward silence and then she noticed her mother and other two sisters looking at her as if she had just said something wrong. "What's wrong with that?" she shouted as she looked around at them.

"How many times a week were y'all having sex before you found out about his cheating?" Joyce asked.

"Once...uhh... sometimes twice," Rená answered.

Her sisters snickered and then burst out laughing.

"Brad would lose his mind if he only got some once or twice a week." Joyce laughed.

"Ernest would too." Sue chuckled.

"What's wrong with that?" Rená snapped. "A woman ain't supposed to let a man jump up and down inside her every night. That's not good for her health."

"Where did you hear that?" Rosa Lee asked with a disturbed look on her face.

"Grandmama told me that the day before my wedding."

"And that's why granddaddy cheated on her for their entire marriage," Sheila interrupted.

"Sheila! Hush your mouth!" Rosa Lee shouted.

"Why? It's the truth, and everybody in here, except Rená, knows about it… even you, Momma."

The room went silent as the women cut their eyes at one another, with each of their expressions confirming Sheila's last statement. They all knew of their grandparent's unspoken secret.

"What are you talking about?" Rená questioned Sheila.

"Are you that naïve?" Sheila stared at Rená with a condescending look. "Don't you remember, grandmama and granddaddy didn't even sleep in the same bed."

"They did that because granddaddy had bad feet and grandmama had arthritis," Rená shot back.

"I guess you are that naïve," Sheila said loud enough for Rená to hear her. "When I was a little girl, I asked grandmamma why didn't she and granddaddy sleep in the same bed like Momma and Daddy, and do you know what she told me?"

"What?" Rená asked as her mother and two other sisters listened with anticipation.

"She said because granddaddy came home one night smelling like spoiled cabbage—" Sheila paused for a moment as Joyce and Sue's laughing interrupted her. "I didn't know what she was talking about back then because I was too young to understand, but now I know."

"That doesn't mean granddaddy was cheating on her," Rená disagreed.

"Why do you think grandmama used to fuss at him for cutting those other women's yards for free? She wasn't fussing at him for being nice. And think about all those times we ran into granddaddy at the grocery store with those younger women from the church. He wasn't passing out no free rides and they didn't have Uber thirty years ago."

"Sheila! That's enough." Rosa Lee stood to her feet pointing her finger at Sheila. "That's my father you're talking about."

"Momma, I loved granddaddy. May God rest his soul, but the truth is the truth," Sheila stated.

"Are you trying to say that Kevin cheated on me because I wasn't giving him enough sex?"

"I'm not *trying* to say nothing. That's exactly what I'm saying. If you don't give him what he wants, then another woman will."

"So how much sex are we supposed to have?" Rená asked as she looked around at her sisters.

"As much as he wants," Joyce answered.

"I give Ernest sex every time he wants it," Sue chimed in.

"What about you, Momma? What do you have to say?" Rená asked.

Her mother hesitated for a second. She didn't feel comfortable discussing her sex life with her daughters. But she looked around and realized that her little girls were all grown women with husbands, so she decided to take part in the conversation. "For the most part, I give it to your daddy whenever he wants it, and it's more than twice a week," she said with a bashful smile.

"And what about you, Sheila?"

"As long as Elton takes care of me and the kids, he can get it any time he wants it. I don't even care if I'm on my period."

"Ugh...girl, that's nasty." Rená cringed and then she looked around the room and noticed that the facial expressions of her mother and other two sisters didn't change. "Have all of y'all done it while y'all were on your cycle?" she asked.

Her mother and sisters quietly nodded.

"Ugh...that ain't right." Rená frowned at them.

"Girl, you ain't talkin' bout nuthin'." Sheila snapped her fingers. "If Elton wants to do it while I'm on my period, I'm going to take my tampon out, lay that towel down on the bed and give him all the bloody coochie he wants," she said as she laughed along with Joyce and Sue.

"You're crazy," Rená said, cracking a smile and shaking her head.

"Sheila might be crazy, but she's right. If you don't take care of your husband, another woman will," Sue warned.

"But I gave him my virginity. He got something no other man ever got." Rená's voice quivered as tears formed in her eyes.

"Okay, I get it. You gave him your virginity on your wedding night, and I'm sure that was something special for both of y'all, but what about the last seventeen years of your marriage? What have you done differently?" Sheila asked.

"Yeah, girl, that virginity mess is overrated," Joyce added. "You can only give a man your virginity one time, and after that, you gotta be able to please him."

"Okay, okay. I get it. I should have been giving Kevin more sex."

"And we ain't talkin' bout that flat backin' old lady type of sex. We talkin' bout that nasty, freaky, porn-star-type sex," Sheila said then jumped up in the middle of the floor and started gyrating her hips and snapping her fingers. "You gotta twerk that thang for your husband."

"Sheila, sit your hot butt down." Rosa Lee playfully popped her twerking daughter on the butt with the back of her hand.

"Hold up, Momma, I got one more question for Rená." Sheila said.

"What is it?" Rená asked.

"How often do you give Kevin head?" she asked with a devious smile on her face.

"NEVER!" Rená shouted with a nasty expression on her face. "I ain't putting his thang in my mouth."

"Are you saying you ain't never—ever gave Kevin no head?" Joyce asked with surprise in her voice. "Not ever for a special occasion."

"Nope, and I never—ever will. Ain't no occasion that special."

"Why not?" Sue asked.

"Because it ain't right. God didn't intend for a man's thang to go in a woman's mouth."

"You're gonna have to show it to me in the Bible where God said that." Sheila challenged.

"Yeah, show it to us in the Bible," Joyce added.

"Y'all leave her alone. That's her business." Rosa Lee tried to defend Rená from Sheila and Joyce's double team.

"Naw, Momma," Sheila raised her voice. "Miss Holy Roller is gon' show us where God said in the Bible that it's wrong to give your husband head."

"It doesn't say it in those words, but a man's thang doesn't belong in a woman's mouth," Rená tried to explain.

"And stop saying thang like we talkin' 'bout a tumor or some abnormal growth. It's a natural part of a man's body. It's a penis, and you better start sucking your husband's, if you want to keep him."

"SHEILA! I told you to watch your mouth." Her mother stood and shouted angrily at her.

"Why Momma? We are all grown women in here, and all of us have husbands," Sheila said then turned to Joyce. "Joyce, do you give Brad head?"

Joyce smiled and nodded.

"What about you, Sue?"

"As long as my husband does me, I don't mind doing him." Sue chuckled.

"And Momma, we know you do it." Sheila laughed.

"How do you know what I do," she snapped.

Sheila cut her eyes at Sue and both started giggling. "Well, one Christmas when we were little girls, me and Sue thought we heard Santa Claus downstairs, so we snuck out of bed to get a look at him, but when we tiptoed halfway down the steps, we saw you giving daddy head on the living room couch."

"And you were working it too." Sue laughed.

"Momma!" Rená said with a shocked look on her face.

"Whatever I do with yo daddy ain't none of y'all business." She cut her eyes at Sheila and Sue.

"Look at you, girl. You're letting your sixty-five-year-old momma out do you," Joyce laughed at Rená.

Rená looked around as her sisters laughed. She even noticed her mother laughing. She didn't know if they were laughing at her, or if they were just enjoying the conversation they were having. But it didn't matter, because she felt she was being ridiculed by her family. They were blaming her for Kevin's infidelity. And she felt guilty. She had let her husband down. Now she questioned whether or not she had been a good wife.

****

Chapter 26

"This is where most men get it wrong. You can't talk a woman into not being mad at you when you're the one that messed up."

-Mrs. Gwendolyn Stokes

Kevin sat at the Stokes' kitchen table enjoying the huge breakfast Mrs. Stokes cooked for him and her husband. Cheese grits, eggs, biscuits, salmon croquettes, and hash browns. Gwendolyn Stokes believed that people had better conversations when their stomachs were full, and she always made sure her houseguests had plenty to eat. *I'd rather have leftovers than not enough* was her motto when it came to cooking. She knew Kevin had a lot to discuss with her husband. He showed up crying at their doorstep at six o'clock this morning.

"The breakfast was delicious, Mrs. Stokes. I'm stuffed," Kevin said as he leaned back in his chair and rubbed his stomach.

"Thank you, and there's plenty more food to eat," she replied.

"Gwen, you know he's a lightweight when it comes to eating." Reverend Stokes laughed as he gobbled down his third helping of eggs and hash browns.

"Maybe later, Mrs. Stokes." Kevin smiled. It felt good to be in the Stokes' house again. This was his first time being there since taking the Pastor's job in Tennessee. He missed these types of moments. He just wished he were here under happier circumstances. A few hours after Rená stormed out of the house with their kids, he got a text from his daughter saying they were headed to Atlanta. Kevin jumped in his car and drove straight there. He wanted to talk to Reverend Stokes in person. FaceTime wasn't going to cut it this time.

"So what do I do now?" Kevin asked Reverend Stokes.

"You wait."

"Wait for what? How can I sit around and do nothing when my wife has just taken my kids and left me?" Kevin asked anxiously. Reverend Stokes didn't give him the answer he was looking for. He was expecting some wise old advice that would instantly solve his marital crisis.

"You've already done enough. Now you must trust God and trust the love Rená has for you," Reverend Stokes said.

"Do you have any advice on what I should say to get her to come back home?" Kevin continued to press.

"You don't understand what I'm saying to you son. Your wife is mad at you. She's hurting, and hearing your voice is the last thing she wants right now. Sometimes, when a woman is angry or upset, the only thing you can do is give her some space and allow her time to be angry. You broke her heart. She has a right to be angry with you."

"That doesn't make any sense" A confused Kevin shook his head.

"Gwen, could you please come and help me over here.' Reverend Stokes beckoned to his wife for assistance.

Right away, Mrs. Stokes stopped washing dishes and dried her hands before sitting at the table with Kevin and her husband. She put her hand on top of Kevin's hand as it rested on the table and began speaking softly to him. "My husband is right. With what your wife is going through, she's going to need a little space. This is where most men get it wrong. You can't talk a woman into not being mad at you when you're the one that messed up. What you need from her is forgiveness, and if she's going to forgive you, it's going to be on her terms and in her own time. When we first got married, I used to hate it when my husband tried to talk me out of my anger. Men don't realize that a woman can love you and be mad at you at the same time. You messed up big time, now give her time to figure out how she wants to deal with it."

"Okay." Kevin nodded his head as he thought about what Mrs. Stokes had just said to him. The advice sounded better coming from a woman.

"What we *really* need to talk about is how you got yourself in this mess in the first place," Reverend Stokes interjected.

"I don't know. It just happened." Kevin lowered his head and shrugged his shoulders.

"You've got to do better than that, son. You don't *just happen* to sleep with five women," Reverend Stokes shot back firmly. He wasn't going to allow Kevin to get off that easily. He knew that if he was going to help him through this rough situation, he was going to have to hear the whole story.

Kevin noticed the serious look on the Reverend's face. He felt like a school kid that had been sent to the principal's office. Reverend Stokes had an intimidating way of reading him that made him nervous.

"Honestly, Reverend, the first time was a mistake. I got caught up in a moment of weakness," Kevin said with a look of hopelessness on his face. "I found myself in the wrong situation at the wrong time and I slipped up...and I hated myself for doing it, but I hated myself even more because I enjoyed it. It felt good to me and before I knew it, I was back for more."

"Sin always feels good when you're doing it, that's why it's so tempting," Reverend Stokes stated. "But in the long run, the consequences aren't worth the momentary gratification."

"Yeah, I know." Kevin lowered his head. "But I was doing so good... I thought I was above committing adultery."

"Why didn't you call me sooner, when all of this drama first started?" Reverend Stokes asked.

"I was too ashamed," Kevin admitted with a heavy burden in his voice. "Besides, I thought I could handle it on my own, but when I slipped up again, I lost myself. I started to feel dirty and unrighteous inside. I didn't feel like I was worthy enough to preach God's word anymore. It felt as if all of God's anointing had been sucked right out of me, and then I began acting according to the way I was feeling inside," Kevin said sadly.

"*As a man thinketh in his heart, so is he...*" Reverend Stokes quoted Proverbs 23:7 to him.

"I felt dirty and unrighteous in my heart and that's how I began acting," Kevin said.

"It sounds like you have a bigger issue than feeling unworthy."

"What do you mean?"

"I'm hearing a self-righteous spirit."

"A self-righteous spirit! What are you talking about?" Kevin's voice shrieked. Reverend Stokes' comment offended him.

"Just listen to what you're saying," Reverend Stokes responded, raising his voice. "You're sitting here telling me that you began to feel unrighteous and unworthy after the first incident. That's telling me that you *felt* righteous and worthy before it happened," Reverend Stokes scolded as he stared at Kevin with his nostrils flared.

Kevin couldn't bear to look into his face. He lowered his head in shame as his beloved mentor continued to chew him out.

"And I'm telling you that God's righteousness ain't no feeling and ain't none of us on this earth worthy enough to preach His Word," Reverend Stokes stressed as he pounded his fist on the table, his anger rising as he continued to talk. He was upset with Kevin for showing symptoms of self-righteousness. He felt Kevin should be past that point after over twenty years in the ministry. "I'm disappointed in you, Kevin. You should know better. It's only by God's grace that we are allowed to preach His Word, and it's only by the blood of Christ that we are declared righteous before Him. It has nothing to do with our feelings."

146

Tears rolled down Kevin's face as he slowly lifted his head and looked into Reverend Stokes' eyes. It troubled him that his mentor was unhappy with him. He also felt embarrassed after realizing that the Reverend's self-righteous diagnosis of him was correct. Kevin thought back on the past twenty years of his life. He had thought that since he stopped selling drugs and doing the things he used to do, that he was a different person. It never occurred to him that deep down he had not been giving Christ the glory for making him a new man.

"What should I do now?" Kevin asked.

"I think you should resign as pastor. I no longer think you're qualified for the position," Reverend Stokes replied.

"I can't resign," Kevin protested as he shook his head in disagreement. In his mind, resigning was the equivalent to quitting and admitting failure, and he had never failed at anything he'd put his mind to.

"If you stay on as the pastor, you will only be staying to serve yourself and not God's people. You cannot be an effective Pastor with a self-righteous spirit. How can you preach the righteousness of God when you don't even know it for yourself?"

"But I do know it. I understand what I have to do. I guarantee you that I won't slip again."

"That's easier said than done. No preacher is above sin. None of us are gods, but the difference is that a self-righteous preacher will wallow in his sins. He doesn't know how to pull himself out because deep down he believes his righteousness is based on his actions. He thinks he's righteous because he's good, and he thinks he's good because he doesn't do the things he used to do," Reverend Stokes said and then he looked Kevin directly in the eyes, "I can't force you to resign, but I will assure you that if you don't, you will fail. And you will find yourself in a much worse situation than you're in now. You'll end up destroying your life and the lives of those people in your congregation... and I can't support that."

Those words infuriated Kevin. He couldn't believe Reverend Stokes threatened not to support him. He lost control and in a fit of anger he said some of the most hateful and disrespectful words he'd ever spoken to his spiritual father before storming out of his house.

Quitting wasn't an option for Kevin and for the first time in over twenty years, he left his mentor's presence feeling fed up and dissatisfied.

Kevin knew Reverend Stokes was serious about not supporting him if he continued to pastor the church in Tennessee. He was upset and angry that he had to choose between pastoring his church and the man that brought him to Christ.

The drive back to Dyersburg was long and dark and filled with tough decisions, and Kevin chose not to resign. He figured that one day he would have to make it in this world without the old man. He knew Reverend Stokes couldn't hold his hand forever. *It's time I step out on my own anyway. All I need is God on my side,* Kevin thought to himself as he drove down the lonely interstate. *I'll show Reverend Stokes that I can do this without him.*

****

Chapter 27

"I'm sorry and I love you."

-Rená Tyler

Rená inched awkwardly down the dark stairs dressed in the sexy new negligee her sisters picked out for her. She stopped at the bottom of the staircase, took a deep breath, and counted to ten. She took another deep breath and whispered to herself. "Come on, Rená. You're a big girl, you can do this."

She had a big surprise for Kevin, and appearing nervous and jittery would only ruin it. She also felt slutty without any panties on, not to mention the slight discomfort of an itching sensation from shaving her lower region completely bare for the first time. But at the moment, none of that mattered. She was determined to please her husband. She adjusted her negligee one more time then strutted into the den where Kevin was kicked back in his recliner reading a book.

Rená had returned from Atlanta earlier that day after being gone for nearly two weeks. And since it was summer break, she left the kids in Georgia with her mother, so she and Kevin could spend some time alone. Despite doing most of their talking and making up via FaceTime, there was still an awkward vibe between them.

Since arriving home a few hours ago, she had spent most of her time upstairs in the bedroom, while Kevin hid downstairs in the den.

Kevin looked up and had to do a double-take when Rená suddenly appeared in the doorway. He sat up in his chair and gazed at her with his mouth locked open. He widened his eyes. His shy and reserved wife was standing in front of him in a red silk negligee with matching red stiletto heels.

"Wow," he mouthed as she walked toward him.

Rená smiled and batted her eyes at his reaction and then she leaned over and gave him a long-wet kiss. Pulling back slowly, she looked into his eyes and whispered, "I'm sorry and I love you."

Kevin didn't understand why she was apologizing to him. *I'm the one that messed up,* he thought. He didn't have a clue she blamed herself for his infidelity.

Kevin's thoughts quickly returned to the moment as he watched his wife slowly push her negligee straps off her shoulders one shoulder at a time. Everything was moving in slow motion as her negligee slid down her arms and dropped to the floor. Kevin bucked his eyes even wider. His once sexually timid wife stood in front of him looking like a porn star, wearing a red laced-bra, with no panties! Her matching garter belt was fastened to red thigh high stockings. But the biggest surprise to Kevin was that her private area had been shaved completely bare.

"Wow, baby... you look gorgeous."

He stood up and circled her a couple of times, looking her up and down to appreciate her from all angles. "Wow, baby!" he said again as he began caressing her all over. He was touching and handling her body as if he was a kid with a new toy.

Rená was nervous at first, but the way Kevin touched and looked at her, gave her confidence, and she was aroused by the way he salivated over her. With her confidence up, she decided to make her move. She pulled his pajamas down, pushed him back into his recliner, and dropped to her knees. Hoping she wouldn't throw up, she took him into her mouth, and tried to remember everything her sisters told her. *"Rule number one, don't let your teeth touch it,"* Sheila stressed. *"Don't use your hands unless it's to gauge your choke limit,"* she remembered Joyce saying, and *"Take your time, don't try to rush,"* was Sue's advice.

As she held him in her mouth and slowly bobbed her head up and down, she thought, *This isn't as bad as I thought it would be. I love my husband enough to do this for him.*

Kevin's breath leaped out of his lungs when her mouth engulfed his manhood. "Rená...What are you..." he tried to speak, but the warm sensation of her mouth stole his words. A single tear formed in the corner of his eye. The thought of his wife loving him enough to go this extra mile overwhelmed him.

After her courageous oral performance, Rená oozed with confidence. She had just conquered her biggest sexual fear. She wanted to turn it up a notch. She calmly grabbed her husband's hand and led him upstairs to their bedroom.

Kevin trailed behind admiring the way her garter belt hugged the top of her butt. And with her six-inch heels on, she was stepping high and hard like a Clydesdale in thick snow, and he was completely captivated.

After laying her down on the bed and taking his time gently kissing all over her body, Kevin positioned himself between her legs and prepared to penetrate her warmth But Rená suddenly stopped him, clasping her legs tightly against his waist, halting his approach.

"What's wrong?" he asked.

Not speaking a word, Rená simply looked into his eyes and surprised him again. She gently placed her hand on the crown of his head and carefully guided his face between her legs. She remembered what Sheila told her. *Don't ever ask a man to go down on you. Just push his head down there, and naturally, he'll act like a dog and start licking.*

She smiled to herself when Kevin didn't ask any questions, nor did he offer any resistance.

For the next two weeks, Kevin and Rená experimented day and night. Like horny teenagers trying every position they could imagine. And even though it was extremely painful, she tried anal sex because he asked her to. She was just glad she paid attention to Joyce when she told her about the breathing exercises that would allow her to relax and endure the initial pain.

Kevin was thoroughly enjoying the new Rená. She was amazing and he appreciated the effort she put forth to please him. He vowed to her and God that he would never cheat on her again.

****

Chapter 28

"If you would have seen me twenty-two years ago, you would have seen a drug-dealing thug. But when God looked upon me back then He saw a preacher, a husband, and a loving father.

-Pastor Kevin Tyler

"WHO CAN FIND A VIRTUOUS WOMAN? FOR HER PRICE IS FAR ABOVE RUBIES."

Pastor Kevin Tyler's voice blasted through the speakers as he looked out at his Sunday morning congregation. "I know today is not Mother's Day, which is when preachers usually preach on this subject, but every day is a day to celebrate not only the virtuous mothers but all the virtuous women in our lives. I have been praying and studying the entire week to bring you a message today about the gifts and callings of God. But when I woke up this morning, I looked over at my beautiful wife, still sound asleep, and I saw the morning light shining on her through our bedroom window, and I just sat there on the side of the bed and stared at her angelic face. It looked like she was glowing, and while I sat there admiring her beauty, God dropped two words in my spirit...He said, *You're welcome...*"

Some of the members of the congregation laughed softly and looked in Rená's direction. She smiled and her cheeks turned red at her husband's narrative.

Kevin gazed affectionately at his wife before continuing his sermon. "I told God, *thank you,* and then I grabbed my Bible, turned to Proverbs 31:10, and read it for the rest of the morning. And I asked myself this question...What does it mean to be a *virtuous woman?* First, I had to go look up the word virtuous, and Webster's dictionary defines virtuous as *displaying virtue.* Then I grabbed my thesaurus off the shelf and searched for synonyms for virtue. Here is what I came up with—decent, ethical, good, honest, just, moral, pure, and righteous. Now after reading all those attributes, I can simply say Rená Tyler and drop the mic. Because she is the epitome of those words."

The congregation burst into laughter, some even stood and clapped, giving Rená a standing ovation.

"Hold up..." Kevin motioned for everyone to settle down and take their seats. "This message I'm getting ready to preach to you is not just about *my* virtuous woman," he emphasized, "but it's about each and every one of you virtuous women sitting here in this building. I admit that God used my lovely wife to inspire me today, but I see strength and virtue in all of you. And not only do I see it but most importantly, God sees it too... Can I tell you all a secret?"

Kevin paused for a second to allow the congregation to reply.

"The secret is that all of you come from a virtuous woman somewhere in your past. Therefore, I can look out at all of you beautiful sisters sitting in here today and honestly say to you... you are all virtuous women... Now I see the way some of you are looking at me, and some of you might say to me, but Pastor Tyler, Sistah So n' So was shakin' it up at the club last night—how can she be virtuous? Another might say to me, but Pastor Tyler, Sistah Such n' Such has four kids by four different men, and she's not married to the man she's living with—how can she be virtuous? And I'll say to them, *IT IS BECAUSE GOD INSTILLED VIRTUE IN THEM,*" Kevin shouted at the top of his lungs.

"If you would have seen me twenty-two years ago, you would have seen a drug-dealing thug. But when God looked upon me back then, He saw a preacher, a husband, and a loving father... All of you beautiful sisters have virtuous attributes instilled in you from hundreds of years of pain and struggle. You have a strength in you far greater than any other group of women on this earth. First of all, it takes real strength and virtue to love us black men, because we can be a handful..."

Kevin paused as some of the women interrupted him. They stood and began clapping and shouting Amen.

"... It takes even more strength and virtue to raise our children all by yourselves. And even then, us black men still don't fully appreciate you for who you are and what you do... Think about this black man... when the world is killing us, hating us, and locking us up in prison by the tens of thousands, who is there to love us? IT'S THE BLACK WOMAN!" Kevin shouted.

"She is *forced* to love the most oppressed group of men on the planet. Let me rephrase that, she *chooses* to love and bear children by the most oppressed group of men on the planet."

Kevin paused again to gauge the different facial expressions peering back at him from the crowded pews. He wanted to make sure he wasn't losing them with his unconventional message.

"Right now, I'm going to ask you all to take a hypothetical trip back in time with me. Let us go about two-hundred years into the past. Now try to visualize what our fore-parents were doing back in 1824. If you can't visualize it, I'm going to help you out, they were slaves right here in The United States of America. Now try to picture this scenario. There is a mean old slave master that goes out and whips one of his strongest and proudest male slaves. He nearly beats him to death, in an attempt to break him. After he has beaten and broken him, he forces him to pick cotton on his plantation every day from sun-up to sundown, and then he tops that off by forcing this broken male slave's wife to pick cotton right beside him from sunup to sundown.

One day, the mean old slave master looks out unto the cotton field and notices that the proud slave man is smiling and having fun while picking cotton next to his beautiful black wife. It infuriated the slave master to see him smiling, so he goes out into the field, and he kicks and beats the male slave in front of his wife. After he beats the slave, he grabs the slave's wife by her hair and begins dragging her toward the big house to do God knows what to her. As the mean old master drags her toward the big house, this strong black woman watches as her husband grips the garden hoe and prepares to defend her, but she makes eye contact with him, she shakes her head and silently mouths *no* to him. She remembered when the slave master sold their two children. Her husband tried to raise up against him and stop him from selling their kids, and master beat him to within an inch of his life. She couldn't bear the thought of losing her children and her husband in the same summer. The male slave obeyed his wife and watched helplessly as old master dragged her into the big house. All he could do was cry and continue to pick cotton...but listen to this," Kevin softens his voice.

"Later that night after being beaten, embarrassed and emasculated in front of his woman, the broken slave returns to the one-room shack he shares with his wife...He is no longer proud. His shoulders are slumped, and his head is hanging low...He's completely broken...But listen to this... when he enters the slave quarters, he finds a hot meal already cooked and waiting for him. His beautiful wife has washed the filth of master off her body. She put on her good dress and made him feel like the man of the house. She never mentioned anything to him about that day. She fed him, obeyed him, and made love to him as if he was her king...She sacrificed her pride for him...THAT'S STRENGHT! THAT'S VIRTUE!" a teary-eyed Kevin shouted to his congregation.

"That same strength and virtue is embedded in each and every one of you. You got it from God by way of your great-great-great grandmothers. They endured so that we black men could survive in this crooked world. So now I'll say back to that person, that Sistah So n' So is just shakin' it up in the club because that's what she thinks her king wants. And Sistah Such n' Such is having babies because she loves her black king so much that she wanted to reproduce with him." Kevin smiled while looking out at the faces of the different women in his congregation.

"I want all the women here today to dig deep and find your strength and virtue. I want you to see in yourselves what God sees in you. And men, look at your queen and see her for who she truly is, recognize that ancient strength and virtue that was instilled in her from the days of old."

After the service, Rená entered Kevin's office and gave him a big hug and a kiss. "I love you, sweetheart," she said with her arms wrapped around his neck. "That was a beautiful sermon."

"I see that kind of strength in you. You are an amazing wife, and I don't deserve you."

"Yes, you do. We deserve each other." She kissed him again.

"No, Rená." Kevin gazed into her eyes. "You have been a wonderful wife to me, and I betrayed you, and even after that, you still go the extra mile to make me happy."

"Shh..." She placed her finger on his lips. "We're not going to speak on the past. Now let's go home and go that extra mile." She smiled at him.

****

Chapter 29

Let thy fountain be blessed: and rejoice with the wife of thy youth. Let her be as the loving hind and pleasant roe; let her breasts satisfy thee at all times; and be thou ravished always with her love.

-Proverbs 5:18-19

"Hello," Kevin answered his phone as he pulled into his driveway.

"Hey!"

"What's up?"

"I enjoyed this morning's sermon."

"Thank you."

"I miss you."

"C'mon, April. I told you we can't do this anymore," Kevin said.

"I thought you loved me."

"I love my wife, and I'm trying to do the right thing."

"CJ has been asking about you. He misses seeing you at night before he goes to bed."

"I'm trying to get things back right with my wife. I'm sorry but I gotta go." Kevin hung up the phone and grabbed the dozen red roses he bought for Rená.

"Wait...Wait...Pastor Tyler!" April cried on the other end of the phone.

**

Two days later

Buzzz! Buzzz!

Kevin picked his cellphone up off his desk and checked the incoming text message. It was from Carmen Jones.

"Haven't seen u n awhile. Do u want 2 meet at my office this evening?"

Carmen

"No, I'm taking Rená out to dinner."

Kevin

"How bout 2morrow?"

Carmen

"Do u remember what I told u last wk...Try n 2 spend more time with the wife."

Kevin

"So no more business meetings?"

Carmen

"I'm afraid not"

Kevin

" ☹ ...smh...gonna miss our rendezvous"

Carmen

****

Chapter 30

"It ain't my place to get in the middle of married folks business."

-Ms. Eddie Mae

Pamela Snipes instinctively opened her eyes at the sound of her husband's truck as he pulled into their driveway. 1:52 flashed bright orange on the digital clock on her nightstand. It always amazed her that she could be sound asleep and oblivious to all the subtle sounds around her, but her internal alarm always woke her at the faintest sound of Parnell's truck. Some nights she could hear him down the street before he even made it to their driveway.

Parnell had been gone all weekend. He got paid Friday afternoon and drove straight to the casinos in Mississippi. Pam could tell by the way he slammed the door and the sound of his footsteps that he lost all his money. She pretended to be asleep when he entered their bedroom, and even though he was intentionally making a lot of noise, she didn't move. She figured that if he knew she was awake, he would try to pick a fight with her, or worse, he would want to have sex. So, she laid still until she heard him snoring. She peeked over at the clock. It was 2:27 A.M., she closed her eyes and exhaled. She only had about three and a half hours before she had to get up and start getting ready for work.

The next morning, Parnell demanded money from Pam. "Let me get twenty dollars," he asked rudely before she walked out of the door to go to work. Even though they worked the same shift at the same factory, she had to leave thirty minutes earlier than him during summer break to drop their three kids off over her mother's house.

"Why don't you just stop by the ATM and get it out of my account?" Pam suggested.

"Damn it, Pam! Are you going to give me the twenty dollars or not? I don't need to hear your lip," he growled.

"Okay, here." She dug in her purse and pulled out a twenty-dollar bill. Parnell quickly snatched the money out of her hand without saying a word.

Pam sensed something wasn't right. Parnell made her give him access to her direct deposit account years ago, and whenever he would blow all his money at the casinos, he would just go to the ATM and take what he needed out of her account. He only asked her for cash when her account was empty, which is impossible because she had just been paid Friday and she hadn't touched her account at all. But her woman's intuition told her to check her account balance anyway. She sat in the parking lot before going into work and accessed her account on her cellphone.

"Ugh..." she gasped and then tears welled in her eyes. Her balance was $3.12, not only did Parnell lose all his money, but he also blew her entire paycheck.

Pam sat in the parking lot and cried before going into work. She wanted to storm into the factory and confront

Parnell about blowing her paycheck, but she knew he would turn it around and find a reason to beat on her She didn't know what to do, so she did the only thing she could do, she prayed and sucked it up. She had already paid the bills at the beginning of the month. Her father taught her to pay all her bills early in the month in case something unexpected happens. The $800 Parnelll blew was her free paycheck. She was going to use it on the kid's school clothes in a couple of months when school started back.

"I'll just work a couple of hours of overtime every day on this pay period," she said to herself as she entered the factory. She was just glad that she always kept a little cash hidden from Parnell. If it wasn't for her stash, she wouldn't know how she was going to feed her kids or keep gas in their vehicles until she got paid again.

After staying over and working a couple of extra hours, Pam stopped by the grocery store to buy pork chops before picking her kids up from her mother's house. She planned on cooking Parnell's favorite dinner tonight, pork chops smothered in onions and gravy with rice and biscuits. She figured it would be a good idea to keep him happy until payday, she knew he didn't have any money and would eventually try to take his frustrations out on her and the children.

Pam picked up her kids and then rushed home to cook dinner and even though she was tired, and her feet hurt from working those extra hours, she had already decided to have sex with him later that night. Everything was going as planned, the pork chops and gravy came out perfect. All she had left to do was to put the biscuits in the oven. Deciding to rest her aching feet while the biscuits baked, Pam set the timer on the oven for eleven minutes. She could feel those extra hours in her feet and back. She flopped down on the couch and relaxed while the biscuits baked.

"Momma wake-up! I smell something burning in the kitchen," Pam's nine-year-old son Jason shook her as she napped on the couch.

Pam jumped to her feet and ran into the kitchen, the timer was buzzing, and the biscuits had burned. Her eleven-minute break had turned into a twenty-five-minute nap.

"I guess I was more tired than I thought," she said to her son as she pulled the charred biscuits out of the oven. She turned the ceiling fan on high and sat the smoking biscuits outside on the back porch.

Parnell made it home about fifteen minutes after Pam and the kids had finished eating. She quickly warmed his food and set his plate on the dining table.

"Here you go, I fixed your favorite." She smiled.

Parnell stared at the plate of food for a few seconds and then he looked at Pam with a frown on his face "What the hell is this?" He asked.

"Pork chops and grav—"

SMACK!

Before Pam could get her answer out, Parnell reached back and slapped the taste out of her mouth. She let out a short scream as she crashed into the wall from the force of the blow.

"You know damn well I can't eat no pork chops and rice with no damn white bread," Parnell huffed as he stood over her.

"I'm sorry... I fell asleep on the couch and accidentally burned the biscuits." A bloodied-mouth Pam tried to explain as she held her hand to her stinging jaw.

"It takes a stupid bitch to burn some biscuits," Parnell shouted and then he snatched her up by her shirt and slapped her down again. "You probably did it on purpose, tryin' to be funny because I lost all my money."

Pam held her hand to her face as she sat on the floor crying. She asked herself, *How could a special meal turn into this.* She knew Parnell was ready to raise hell tonight. He was going to turn this biscuit incident into an all-night event. She had to think fast to prevent the senseless beating that she was about to receive. She quickly pulled herself off the floor and put his plate in the microwave. While Parnell showered, Pam sped to the store to buy a can of biscuits. She was trying her best to prevent a beating.

The store wasn't crowded, and Pam was able to get in and out and back home in under fifteen minutes.

"Where in the hell have you been?" Parnell growled at her as she walked back through the door.

"I ran to the store to get you some biscuits." Her voice trembled. She could tell by his tone that he was ready to start fighting. She sat her car keys and cellphone on the coffee table, and quickly kicked her shoes off her aching feet and hurried to the kitchen to bake his biscuits.

"You must think I'm a fool," Parnell shouted as he followed her to the kitchen.

"What are you talking about?" Pam flinched and braced herself as she turned to answer him.

166

"It don't take that long to run to the store to buy a can of biscuits," he continued to shout.

"I was only gone for fifteen min—"

SMACK!

"OW!" Pam screamed as the back of Parnell's hand hit her with so much force that he knocked her into the refrigerator. The can of biscuits fell out of her hand and burst on the kitchen floor.

Before Pam could regain her bearings from the slap, Parnell hit her again. "Oh…" and again, "Ouch…Parnell, please stop," she begged as she tried to cover her face. She could hear him repeatedly mumbling *stupid bitch* through his clenched teeth as he continued his vicious attack.

Finally, Parnell stopped, but he wasn't done. He stood over her huffing and puffing as if he was the big bad wolf. Pam looked up at him and saw nothing but insane rage in his eyes, and she knew from experience that the little slapping session was not enough to satiate his appetite for violence. Every time he had that look in his eyes, she prayed to God that he would not lose control and accidentally kill her in his fit of rage.

"I'm going to teach you a lesson about sneaking out of this house," Parnell barked and then he grabbed her hair and began dragging her to their bedroom.

Pam screamed and kicked as she dug her fingernails into his hands in an attempt to loosen the grip he had on her hair. She knew she had to keep the fighting out of the bedroom. As long as they were outside of the bedroom, he would simply beat on her, but in the privacy of their bedroom, he would not only beat her, but he would also torture and rape her too.

"Daddy, please stop hurting Momma!" Their son Jason screamed as he ran into the hallway with tears in his eyes.

"Daddy, please stop!" Patricia, their eleven-year-old daughter, cried while holding her five-year-old brother Parnell Jr.'s hand, who cried loudly.

"Get y'all asses back in your rooms," Parnell roared at the top of his lungs.

Parnell Jr. instantly ran and hid in the closet at the sound of his father's voice, but Jason and Patricia stood their ground, and with tears in their eyes, they begged for their mother's life.

Pam had never seen her kids react this way to her and Parnell's fighting. Normally they would close their bedroom doors and cry until the ordeal was over. She looked into their eyes and felt ashamed. She didn't want them to see her like this anymore.

"Y'all go to your rooms," she ordered them with a calm voice. "I'm going to be alright," she lied. She was saying what she needed to say to get them out of harm's way. She was afraid for their safety. She didn't know how Parnell was going to react to their act of defiance.

But her kids wouldn't leave, they looked at her as she sat on the floor with a bloody mouth while their father gripped a hand full of her hair. They were getting too old to cower in their rooms while their mother was being beaten.

And at that very moment, while looking into her children's eyes, Pam had had enough. Her eyes opened to her reality, and she realized she had to get her kids *and* herself out of this toxic situation. But before she could say another word to her two little brave soldiers, Parnell released her hair. He pushed the two kids into the bedroom and slammed the door and wolfed his threat to them. "If y'all come out of that room, I'm going to whoop y'all asses."

Pam seized her opportunity and before Parnell could turn around and focus his rage back on her, she quickly hopped up off the floor and bolted out the front door. Barefoot and scared, Pam ran as fast as she could. Parnell tried to give chase, but he was too slow and too out of shape as her old skills as a high school track runner kicked in.

As she made her escape and left Parnell chasing her dust, Pam felt a sense of freedom and power she hadn't felt since before she was married. She couldn't believe this was her first time running from a beating. She ran for her life. She left her phone, her shoes, and her kids behind, but as she ran down the long dark street, she was already trying to figure out how to get her kids out of that house.

Once she lost Parnell, Pam doubled back to the other side of the street. She tipped through her neighbor's back yards until she made it to Ms. Eddie Mae's house

Ms. Eddie Mae was the nosey old lady that lived directly across the street from Pam. She was a recluse that rarely spoke to anyone. All the kids in the neighborhood were afraid of her. She would peek out of her window or sit on her porch and forbid them from cutting through her yard. But Pam had noticed something strange about her neighbor over the years.

Ms. Eddie Mae would only speak to her the mornings following one of Parnell's beatings. She would simply say to her, "*Hey, honey, are you all right,*" and Pam would nod her head yes and go about her day.

Pam carefully tipped through the backyard and stepped to the backdoor with caution. She was nervous and scared. She had never seen any visitors over Ms Eddie Mae's house, and she didn't know how she was going to react to her knocking on her backdoor without any shoes on, but she couldn't turn around, not now. She had her kids on her mind.

When Pam raised her fist to knock on the door, Ms Eddie Mae suddenly swung the door open as if she had been expecting her.

"Come on in, baby." She smiled at Pam. "Are you all right?"

"Yes, ma'am," Pam replied as she stepped inside.

"I saw you running out of the house. Child, I didn't know those wide hips and big thighs could move that fast. It's about time. You should have run away from that boy a long time ago." Ms. Eddie Mae chuckled.

"So, you know what's been going on?" Pam asked shamefully.

"Yeah, baby... I know that boy has been jumping on you for years."

"Why didn't you say anything to me about it?" Pam asked.

"It ain't my place to get in the middle of married folks' business," Ms. Eddie Mae said, and then she walked into the kitchen and poured Pam a glass of water. She continued talking to Pam as she walked back into the living room with the water. "Besides, you weren't ready to leave him, but now that Pastor Tyler has been tipping around over there, things have changed for you."

Pam looked embarrassed when she mentioned Pastor Tyler's name.

"Don't look at me like you're ashamed. I ain't judging you. But I've noticed how happy you've been since he's been coming over."

"Do you have a phone I can use?" Pam asked, quickly cutting her off. She didn't have time to talk about Pastor Tyler, the only thing on her mind was getting her kids out of that house.

Pam peered at her house through the living room window. Surprised by the view. The window was just the right height and sat at the perfect angle to see directly into her bedroom window. She saw a pair of binoculars sitting on the coffee table, and then it dawned on her how Ms. Eddie Mae seemed to know when Parnell had been hitting on her. She wondered what else she had seen going on in her bedroom.

Ms. Eddie Mae passed Pam her phone and she quickly dialed her daughter's number.

"Hello."

"Patricia! This is your mother," Pam said to her daughter. "Where are your brothers?"

"We are all in my room," Patricia whispered into her cellphone as she listened for her father's footsteps.

"Listen carefully to what I'm about to say." Pam paused before giving her daughter instructions. "I need y'all to put your clothes and shoes on and get in the bed under the covers and pretend to be asleep because as soon as your daddy leaves again, I'm gonna come and get you and your brothers."

"Momma, no!" Patricia cried.

"What's wrong, sweetheart?"

"Daddy said he's going to kill you when he finds you. I think he's for real this time," she whimpered.

"Don't worry about that, baby. I'm coming to get you and your brothers. Now do as I say. I love you."

"Okay, Momma. I love you too."

Pam peeked through Ms. Eddie Mae's window and watched as Parnell's truck zoomed up and down the street, circling the block like a hungry shark. She could hear his rage revving through the truck's engine and the red brake lights on the truck reminded her of his anger-filled eyes. He would torture her if he caught her. She thought about the advice her First Lady gave her a few months ago, *"The next time he puts his hands on you, you should call the police."*

She planned to call the police, but first, she had to get her kids out of the house. No matter how bad a monster Parnell was, he was still her children's father, and she didn't want her kids to see their father being dragged away in handcuffs and thrown into the back of a police car.

After nearly twenty-minutes of surveilling her house from Ms. Eddie Mae's living room window, Pam noticed Parnell's truck was no longer circling the block. This was her opportunity to get her kids. She carefully eased out of the front door. She looked both ways then sprinted across the street to her kids.

"Y'all get up, c'mon let's go," Pam said in a loud whisper as she rushed through her daughter's bedroom door. "Baby, why aren't you dressed?" She asked when she noticed Parnell Jr. was still in his blue Sesame Street pajamas.

"I tried to get him ready, but he was so scared of Daddy that he wouldn't let me change his clothes," Patricia explained to her mother.

She didn't have time to dress her son, she grabbed a change of clothes and picked him up in her arms. Before leaving the house, she snatched her cellphone off the coffee table and stuck her feet in her shoes. Pam and her kids looked both ways and then dashed across the street to Ms. Eddie Mae's house.

Now that she had gotten her kids out of the house, Pam decided it was time to call for help. She called First Lady Rená Tyler.

"Hello."

"Hey, First Lady, this is Pamela Snipes."

"Hey, Sistah Pam. How are you?"

"I need your help."

"What can I do for you?" Rená asked, hearing the desperation in Pam's voice.

Pam quickly narrated her situation to Rená before explaining to her how she could help. "Can you come pick up me and my kids? I can't get in my car, nor can I go to my mother or sister's house because Parnell will find me."

"I'm sorry, Sistah Pam, but I'm in Atlanta picking up my kids."

"Oh...Okay..." Pam paused for a moment. "Thank you anyway. I'll figure something else out."

Rená detected the disappointment in Pam's voice. She felt guilty because she had promised Pam, she would be there for her whenever she decided to leave her husband

"Wait a minute," Rená shouted into the phone stopping Pam before she hung up. "I'll call Kevin to pick you up. He's still in Dyersburg."

****

Chapter 31

O wretched man that I am! Who shall deliver me from the body of this death?

-Romans 7:24

Kevin was at home asleep in his lazy boy recliner when Rená called and asked him to pick up Pam and her kids. He refused and reminded her of their agreement that he would not deal with any female members without her being present. But Rená felt a sense of responsibility for Pam and her kids. She had promised Pam she would be there for her if she needed her.

"Kevin, please do this one little favor for me. I gave her my word that I would help her whenever she decided to leave her husband," Rená pleaded.

"I just don't think it's a good idea," Kevin replied.

"Please, baby, if you do this for me, I'll try to do that three-point-special you were talking about the other night," Rená said in her sexy voice. She had been married to Kevin for over seventeen-years. But it had only been in the past few weeks she realized she could manipulate him with sex.

Kevin couldn't resist the idea of a three-point-special and quickly gave in. He stayed on the phone with Rená until he pulled up in front of Ms. Eddie Mae's house, and as soon as he saw Pam walking toward his car, he thought about Reverend Stokes' warning, *God ain't gonna bless no lie.* He couldn't help but feel some regrets. If he had come clean about all his affairs, including he and Pam's, Rená would not have called him from Atlanta and put him in such a precarious situation. Though he had been faithful for the past few weeks, He knew it was not a good idea for him to be in the car with Pam.

Once he picked Pam and her kids up, Kevin made sure he sent Rená a play-by-play text of every move they made. He dropped Pam's kids off over her mother's house and drove her straight to the Dyersburg Police Department. She filed a complaint and took out a restraining order against her husband. The police arrested Parnell that same night, and they assured her that he would not be able to get out on bail until the next afternoon, which would give her time to pack all of her and her kid's things.

After leaving the police station, Kevin drove Pam back to her house. The excitement of the night had waned, and now it was time for him to drop her off and go their separate ways. As he turned on to her street and drove closer to her house, he prayed in his mind for the strength to resist the temptation of her flesh.

Kevin pulled into Pam's driveway and shifted his car in park. He could feel the sexual energy between them. *Be strong, Kevin,* he said in his mind as he held his breath. He intentionally tried not to look at her as they sat inside of his parked car. He felt like a benevolent vampire trying to resist the call of an innocent young girl's pulsating jugular. His heart thumped with intensity as he cut his eyes down at her thighs. They looked so juicy and mouthwatering to him. It seemed as if he could smell her erotic aroma seeping through her pores. She was vulnerable right now and would willfully accept the comfort of his shepherd's rod as if it were a gift sent directly from heaven. He began thinking about how wildly she squirmed and moaned as if every orgasm she got was her first.

"Thank you, Pastor Tyler," Pam said as she cracked the passenger side door, causing the interior light to shine, illuminating her voluptuous body.

"You're welcome," he replied as he tried to keep his eyes from drifting down.

She paused before getting out. "Do you want to come in for a few minutes?" she asked with a hint of seduction in her voice.

Kevin thought hard and considered her proposition for a moment, but he dug deep and found the strength to resist. "Nah, I think I'll pass. I'm trying to change some things in my life too."

"Are you sure?" she asked as she reached over into his lap and caressed the erection bulging through his pants. "It looks like you can use some attention."

"Yes I can, but I'd better get home. I'm trying to do right by my wife."

"I can respect that," she said, and then she kissed him on the cheek and got out of the car.

Kevin watched Pam as she made it into her house safely, and then he pulled off in a hurry before he changed his mind. He praised and thanked God all the way home for giving him the strength to resist the urge to have sex with Pam. He felt like his life was finally getting back on track. "Glory Hallelujah," he shouted as he drove down the quiet streets of Dyersburg. He was so excited that he even began crying and speaking in *Tongues.*

After making it home, Kevin called his wife to tell her goodnight and to express how much he loved her. He took a quick shower and jumped into bed, but he could not sleep. He tossed and turned. His mind kept drifting off on thoughts of sex. Rená had only been gone for two days, and she wouldn't be back until Saturday evening, which was four days away. The sexual urges still lingered from being in the car with Pam earlier that night. He didn't know how he was going to make it until Saturday without sex. He thought about how Ms. Cindy used porn to ease her sexual frustrations. He picked up his phone and thought about searching for a porn site, but he quickly cast those thoughts away. Instead, he searched for sermons on YouTube. He needed to hear a word from God.

Ding Dong!

Ding Dong!

Ding Dong! Ding Dong!

The sound of the doorbell interrupted Kevin as he prepared to watch sermons. "Who could be ringing my doorbell at this time of night?" he said to himself as he made his way to the door.

He was surprised when he looked at the door camera and saw Pam standing outside in a bathrobe and slides. Thinking something was wrong, he quickly opened the door. "Hey, Pam. Is everything alright?"

"No, it's not," she replied anxiously as she stepped through the door and rushed past him.

"What's going on? Why are you here?" he asked as he stood with the door open.

"I can't stay at my house tonight. I keep thinking Parnell is going to walk through the door."

"Do you want me to get you a hotel room?"

"No, I don't want a hotel room. I was thinking that since First Lady is in Atlanta, I could stay here with you tonight?"

"I don't think that would be a good idea," Kevin said nervously, while still holding the door open.

"But, Pastor Tyler, I need you tonight," Pam said with desperation in her voice. She moved in close to him, wrapped her arms around his neck, and began kissing his cheek and licking his ear. "I need you more tonight than I ever have before," she whispered in his ear.

"I can't." Kevin gently pushed her back. "We can't do this," he said as he backed away and looked into her eyes. It took every ounce of his will power to push her away. But he had to remain strong for the sake of his marriage.

"But I need you to make me feel good," Pam begged. She untied her robe and dropped it to the floor. She wasn't wearing anything underneath. Kevin's chin dropped at the sight of her naked body. Shocked by her boldness, he didn't move as she eased toward him. She pushed the door closed and locked it. She turned to him and carefully wrapped her arms around his neck and planted soft wet kisses on him, while whispering between each kiss. "Pastor, please make me feel good... make me feel the way you did the first time you came to my house... please... make me moan... I want to feel you inside of me." She purred like a kitten as she begged him to make love to her.

Kevin tried to resist, but his will was weakening with every soft kiss and with each whisper from her lips.

Help me, God, he prayed in his mind. *Please stop me Lord. I don't want to do this.*

Kevin's mind was losing the battle against his flesh as he felt the warmth of Pam's naked body pressed against him. Struggling at the moment, he thought about the words of Jesus "...*Indeed the spirit is willing, but the flesh is weak.*" He took a deep breath and closed his eyes as he surrendered to his desires. And like air being let out of a balloon, Kevin felt all his strength and willpower abandoning him as he exhaled, and in a split second of weakness, he wrapped his arms around Pam, gripping as much of her plump naked behind as his hands could hold. A single tear rolled out of the corner of his eye, as his mind admitted defeat, and he surrendered to his flesh.

At that very moment of his surrender, Romans 7:14-24 flashed through his mind, and after over twenty years as a born-again believer, he had finally found himself experiencing first-hand the conflict the Apostle Paul spoke of in those verses.

7:14-15 I am carnal sold under sin. For that which I do I allow not: for what I would, that do I not, for what I hate, that I do... Kevin hated that he could not resist the fleshly temptation in front of him. He loathed himself for being so weak and helpless because at this moment, he was about to do the very thing he swore to God and his wife he would never do again.

7:16-17 *If then I do that which I would not, I consent unto the Law that it is good. Now then, it is no more I that do it, but sin that dwelleth in me...* Kevin felt the lust and passion burning deep inside his flesh as he kissed Pam's lips. And as their bodies melted together, his mind still screamed no. But he could not stop his hands from squeezing her thickness nor his mouth from tasting her lips.

7:18-20 *For I know that in me (that is, in my flesh,) dwelleth no good thing: for to will is present with me; but how to perform that which is good I find not. For the good that I would, I do not: but the evil which I would not, that I do. Now if I do that I would not, it is no more I that do it, but sin that dwelleth in me.* Kevin's conscience begged him to stop as he led Pam upstairs to his bedroom. He felt possessed as his mind watched helplessly while his body continued to do what he did not want it to do.

7:20-23 *For I delight in the law of God after the inward man: But I see another law in my members, warring against the law of my mind, and bringing me into captivity to the law of sin which is in my members.* As he laid Pam's steaming hot body down on his bed, he prayed in his mind and made one last feeble attempt to halt the sinful actions his flesh had put into motion.

I am a man of God, I can stop this, he tried to encourage himself. And then he prayed. *In the mighty name of Jesus, I command these feelings of lust to go away.* But nothing happened. There was no voice from heaven, no sudden flash of light, no boost of power, and

Kevin found himself completely naked crawling on top of Pam's body.

7:24 *O wretched man that I am! Who shall deliver me from the body of this death?* Kevin closed his eyes and plunged deep inside of Pam's flesh.

An hour later, while Pam lay sound asleep in his wife's bed, Kevin snuck into the bathroom and cried for his soul and his marriage.

****

Chapter 32

Beware of Delilah...

-Pastor's Book of Warnings

Tiffany and Mary stood whispering to each other down the hall from the pastor's office. Mary's older sister Susie was now in charge of cleaning the pastor's office. Linda Green had passed the duties to her after her confrontation with Pastor Tyler.

"How do I look?" Tiffany asked.

"Thick to death," Mary giggled. "He can't turn all of that down."

The two girls had devised a plan to try to seduce Pastor Tyler. Mary convinced her sister to let her clean the office for the summer. To help her stay busy before going away to college. It was Tiffany's idea, so she decided to go first.

Tiffany was the youngest daughter of Ray and Linda Green. She had just graduated from Dyersburg High school, and she planned to attend Middle Tennessee State University in the fall. Like most teens, Tiffany spent most of her time on social media. She was no prude, but she wasn't the most sexually experienced either. Since losing her virginity at sixteen, she'd been mildly active.

She and her best friend, Mary Armstrong, had a crush on Pastor Tyler. They'd been infatuated with him since the day they noticed he was wearing a pair of $1400 Christian Louboutin boots. From then on, the two would sit in church on their cellphones looking up the price of every piece of clothing he'd wear. His style and sophistication fascinated them.

Kevin had been in his office trying to study when thoughts of what he and Pam had done a few weeks ago continued to plague his conscience. Romans 7:24 was on constant rotation in the back of his mind and he couldn't seem to make it stop. *O wretched man that I am! Who shall deliver me from the body of this death?* He had fallen completely off the wagon. He'd recently resumed his extramarital affairs with both April and Carmen, while also recruiting additional female members of the congregation to his roster.

Kevin was headed in a downward spiral. It seemed as if his sexual appetite was never satisfied. He'd have sex with one of the many women and feel terrible about it, but the only thing that would numb the feeling was more sex, leaving him feeling depressed once again. It was a vicious cycle.

His depression had gotten so bad that he even began to contemplate suicide. Fasting and prayer wasn't working. His sins had completely consumed him. And since Rená's sexual appetite had also increased, he'd even begun to rely on the help of Viagra to keep up with everyone's sexual needs. His life had gotten completely out of hand.

"Hey, Pastor Tyler." Tiffany startled him as she suddenly appeared in the doorway of his office.

"Hi." Kevin lifted his head. "Um...Uh...Tiffany, right?" He guessed at her name.

"You got it right. I'm surprised you remember my name."

"I know who you are. I know all of my members. You're Sistah Green's daughter. My wife and I sent you a present for your high school graduation last month."

"Oh, yeah. Thanks for those Air Pods." She smiled.

"You're welcome. Now, what can I do for you?" Kevin asked.

"I'm here for Sistah Susie. Her back is bothering her again, and she asked me to come down here and clean your office for her."

"Give me a second to gather my things, and I'll be out of your way," Kevin said as he fumbled with some papers on his desk.

"Hold up for a minute." Tiffany pulled out her cellphone and started playing with the screen. "Let me see... D&G button-down $670...Umm...brown D&G slacks $575...and D&G loafers—Ooh! $1375...Umph Pastor, you spent big money on those shoes."

"What are you doing?" Kevin chuckled.

"I'm pricing your outfit, and so far, you're wearing about $2600 worth of Dolcé & Gabbana." She smiled as she continued looking him over and playing with her phone. "What kind of watch is this?" she asked as she grabbed his wrist.

"You are a crazy little girl." Kevin smiled as he pulled his wrist away from her grip.

She gave him a sassy look. "I'm not a little girl anymore. I turned eighteen two months ago. I'm a grown woman now," she said saucily and popped her neck.

"You're still just a baby compared to me," Kevin teased and laughed at her.

"Humph...I ain't no baby. You can't fit all of this in no diaper," Tiffany said as she turned to the side, grabbed one of her butt cheeks and popped it, causing it to bounce and jiggle like Jello.

Kevin instantly erased the smile from his face and his voice took on a more serious tone. "Okay, Tiffany. I'm going to leave on that note." He quickly grabbed his briefcase and walked toward the door.

"Wait a minute, Pastor Tyler." Tiffany stepped in front of him to block his path. "What did I do? Why are you suddenly acting funny towards me?"

"Because what you just did was extremely inappropriate."

"If shaking my booty is inappropriate, then what do you call what you and April are doing?"

"What are you talking about?" Kevin asked nervously, shocked by what she had just said to him.

"I babysit for her sometimes, and she told me all about y'all little sexual relationship."

"I don't know what you are talking about," Kevin tried to lie.

"You don't have to lie to me. I ain't goin' to put you and April's business out there like that."

"April and I don't have any business for you to put out there."

But Tiffany wasn't buying it, and now that she had built up her courage, she was determined to seduce him. "I'll tell you what, Pastor Tyler. Let's just forget about what I just said about April." She stood in front of him and looked up into his eyes, and then she put her hand on his chest and gently pushed him back as she moved forward. "Have a seat so we can talk," she said, while pushing him back onto the black leather couch across from his desk.

"What do we have to talk about?" Kevin asked as he plopped down on to the couch.

Tiffany began nervously pacing in her spandex shorts. Kevin noticed how her booty bounced with every step she took. He felt those lustful urges boiling inside him, and he couldn't stop looking at her body. His manhood swelled as he pictured her firm cheeks bouncing against his pelvis.

"I'm going to be straight up and honest with you, Pastor Tyler." Tiffany timidly began to speak. "I've been crazy about you ever since you came to this church. You're smooth, you dress good, you got a nice body and even though you are in your forties, you're sexier than most of the younger guys around here. I know you're married, and we can't be in no relationship, but I'm going away to college soon." She paused and walked over and closed the door to his office and locked it. "I just want to be with you one time before I go, and I promise you, I ain't gon' tell nobody."

Her proposal flattered Kevin, which made him want her even more. He still couldn't take his eyes off her white spandex shorts. Hypnotized by the way they hugged her thighs, he took a deep breath and tore his eyes away from her mid-section long enough to look in her face. "Do you promise not to say a word to anyone? You know your mother would kill me if she found out about this," he said.

"I promise, I won't tell a soul," Tiffany said as she peeled her shorts and panties off.

Kevin's heart thumped wildly, and his mouth watered at the sight of Tiffany's neatly shaved flesh. He gave her a look of submission, and she straddled him as he sat on the couch. They began kissing as he squeezed her delicate young body.

For the rest of the summer, Tiffany cleaned the Pastor's office at least twice a week. She instantly broke her promise to him by telling her best friend Mary Armstrong all the juicy details of their sexual encounter

****

Chapter 33

"Beware of the Forbidden Fruit..."

-The Pastor's Book of Warning

Choir practice had been over for nearly an hour. Deron Jackson turned the power off to all the music equipment. He sat down on the stool in front of his giant Yamaha keyboard and looked around the empty church. Deron was New Hope's twenty-five-year-old music director, and part of his weekly routine was hanging around the church on Thursday nights after choir practice ended. His personal life was boring. There wasn't much of a social scene for the LGBTQ community in Dyersburg.

Finding love seemed impossible for him. Of course, there was the occasional fling with a man who was on the "down-low," but he wanted more. Deron hadn't had a real relationship since college, and he longed for a genuine connection with someone. And even though meaningless sex wasn't his favorite kind of sexual activity, it was better than nothing.

At times, Deron found himself questioning God about his sexuality. He figured his life would be less complicated if he were straight. In addition to having zero communication with his father and a huge deficit in the relationship department, he also had to endure the self-righteous hypocrites of the church judging him from their high horses. When the previous pastor hired him as music director, some of the members were so appalled about his decision that they found new church homes.

Deron was nervous when Pastor Tyler came from Atlanta to fill the available pastor's position. He was concerned that he might have a problem with his sexuality. But that wasn't at all the case. He was thankful for how progressive Pastor Tyler was and appreciated his teachings of inclusion no matter a person's sexual orientation. In his church, everyone had the right to serve and worship God.

Deron turned all the lights off in the church and started to leave when he noticed the light still on in the Pastor's office. It shined through the bottom of the door in the dark sanctuary. Assuming Pastor Tyler had forgotten to turn it off, he stepped into the office to hit the switch. But Pastor Tyler startled him when he opened the door. He was behind his desk looking at his laptop.

"Oh, excuse me, Pastor Tyler. I'm sorry for bursting in on you. I didn't think anyone was in here," Deron apologized.

Kevin jumped when the door suddenly swung open. Clearly surprised, he tried to play it cool. "Don't worry about it. I was just finishing some work," he said as he slammed his laptop closed. He didn't want Deron to see the porn video playing on the screen. The effect of the Viagra pills he had been taking kept him aroused. He had gotten so bad, that if he wasn't having sex, he was either watching it or plotting to get it.

"Are you okay, Pastor?" Deron asked. He noticed Kevin looked flush and tiny beads of sweat dotted his forehead.

"Yes, I'm okay." Kevin shifted uncomfortably in his chair, trying to hide that his pants were unzipped, and he was fully exposed behind his desk.

Deron scanned the office and noticed an open jar of Vaseline on the desk next to the laptop. He looked back at the beads of sweat on his Pastor's forehead and then back at the laptop and Vaseline. It suddenly dawned on him what his Pastor was doing in his office this late in the evening.

"I'm sorry for disturbing you," he said nervously as he turned to walk out the door.

Kevin saw the look in Deron's eyes and knew he figured out what he was doing in his office. "Wait a minute, Deron. Don't leave yet," Kevin said as he quickly zipped his pants, confirming Deron's suspicion. "Come in and close the door. I need to have a word with you."

Kevin didn't know if it was the porn clip he had just watched or the effects of the Viagra he had taken earlier, but his lower region throbbed at the sight of Deron's butt in his skinny jeans. He didn't know where the thoughts were coming from. *I'm not gay,* he thought to himself. He had lived in Atlanta, which was the black gay capital of the world for years and he had never been attracted to a man. But for some strange reason, tonight, Deron aroused him.

"Why are you here so late?" Kevin asked. "Choir practice was over more than an hour ago."

"There's just not much for me to do in Dyersburg. So I like to hang back and be alone," Deron replied.

Kevin stood and walked from behind his desk. Deron could clearly see the effect of the Viagra bulging through his pants.

"What are you doing, Pastor Tyler?" he asked in a panicked tone while shifting his eyes. He stood frozen as Kevin walked behind him.

"I just want to check you out," Kevin said as he eased closer and began fondling his butt.

"Wa... wait a minute, Pastor Tyler. I don't think this is appropriate."

"Shh...just go with the flow. I'm gonna give you something to do tonight," Kevin whispered in his ear.

Deron turned around and tried to kiss him, but Kevin pushed him away. "I wanna have sex with you, but I ain't gonna kiss no man," he said. He unzipped his pants, pulled out his manhood, and grabbed the jar of Vaseline off the desk. "Now turn back around and pull your pants down," he commanded.

Deron didn't say another word. He understood the assignment. He simply obeyed his pastor's demand and assumed the position. This scene had become all too familiar to him. Pastor Tyler just wanted a quickie with no-strings-attached, which was more than what he would have gotten tonight had he not walked into the office.

****

Chapter 34

*"Lord have mercy, Jesus! Who else has been sleepin'
with the Pastor?"*

- Marilyn Golden

April could barely contain her excitement. One of her biggest dreams was about to come true. She was on her way to the *Woman Evolved* conference. She and about a dozen women from the church were taking the minibus to Dallas. She had been sending posts to her friends since she woke up that morning. April planned to chronicle the entire experience on social media, including the drive to Texas. She took a picture of Carmen Jones and posted it with the caption, *A strong woman in the Lord.*

Carmen and the church secretary, Jackie, were sharing the driving responsibilities. The praise and worship leader, Marilyn Golden, volunteered to lead the group of women in prayer before they departed. She stood at the front of the bus and asked that everyone lower their heads.

"Heavenly Father, we pray that you will protect us as we travel these dangerous highways. Keep us safe and secure as we depart from our loved ones, and Lord, we ask that you watch over our families while we're gone. In your Son, Jesus' name, we pray, Amen.

"Amen," all the women repeated in unison.

"Uuugghhh," Tiffany Green began crying aloud immediately after the prayer. Everyone turned and stared curiously at her as her wailing continued to get louder and louder.

"Tiffany! What's wrong with you?" Linda asked her distraught daughter.

"I can't go with y'all," Tiffany cried.

"Baby, what's going on?" Marilyn asked.

Tiffany's crying continued for a few more seconds before she calmed down enough to speak. Her wailing had turned into loud sobs and intense chest heaves. She timidly looked around the bus at all the eyes that were locked on her.

"I'm pregnant," she whimpered as she lowered her head and shrunk in her seat.

"PREGNANT?" Linda shouted. "Who's the daddy?"

Tiffany paused and nervously looked around at everyone on the bus as they all stared at her with anticipation. "Pastor Tyler," she muttered as she tried to shrink even lower into her seat.

"PASTOR TYLER!" Linda shouted out at her. She stood to her feet with her anger-filled eyes peering down at her frightened daughter.

Tiffany, now quivering in her seat, peeked up at her mother, and started bawling aloud again.

The entire bus seemed to gasp at the same time. They were all stunned by Tiffany's shocking revelation.

"Lord have mercy," Marilyn shouted as she lowered her head and shook it with disappointment. Her voice pierced through the eerie silence that overtook the bus as the women tried to process what Tiffany had just said.

"Did she say Pastor Tyler?"Susie whispered in disbelief as she stared at Tiffany.

"Oh no, Pastor...What have you done?" Jackie said under her breath.

"Let us off this bus. We're goin' to tell your father," Linda grabbed Tiffany's arm and snatched her out of her seat.

Suddenly, everyone turned and looked at April as she burst into tears and cried.

"What's wrong with you?" Marilyn asked.

"I've been sleeping with Pastor Tyler too. I thought I was the only one. He told me he loved me."

"Lord, have mercy, *Jesus*! Who else has been sleepin' with the Pastor?" Marilyn shouted out in frustration.

Dottie Ann raised her hand slowly.

Tiffany's best friend Mary Armstrong eased her hand up. Her older sister Susie quickly nudged her in the ribs. "Mary Lee put your hand down," she snapped at her. "I guess Pastor Tyler is the mystery man you've been bragging about."

Mary instantly dropped her hand and lowered her head.

Pamela Snipes raised her hand proudly. "I knew I wasn't the only one having sex with him, but I'm good with it. Pastor Tyler gave me the confidence I needed to leave my husband."

"Me too," Barbara Jo added. "If it wasn't for me foolin around with Pastor Tyler, I would still be wasting my time in a dead marriage."

"Let's go, Tiffany. I'm calling your father right now," Linda said as she pulled her cell phone out.

"Ladies, we don't have time for this. We're going to be behind schedule if we don't leave soon," Carmen Jones yelled. She was upset too. She thought Pastor Tyler was her personal boy toy. She had no idea he was having sex with so many other women. She looked around at the different faces sitting on the bus and shook her head at them for telling their business. She may have been having an affair with Pastor Tyler, too, but she wasn't foolish enough to confess it in front of a bus full of gossiping women. She had a husband and a reputation to protect.

"We're not going to Dallas," Linda said while dragging Tiffany off the bus.

"I'm not going either," April said somberly with tears in her eyes. Her big day was ruined and her dream of experiencing the Women's conference had been destroyed. She looked down at her phone and then shook her head before storming off the bus.

"I can't do this either." Dottie Ann got up out of her seat and walked off the bus.

"I can't support this." Marilyn shook her head and threw her hands in the air before exiting the bus.

"I'm sorry, but our trip is canceled." Jackie stood and reluctantly announced to the handful of stunned women that were left sitting on the bus.

****

Chapter 35

"I'm sorry First Lady, but me and Pastor Tyler have been messin' around for almost two months, and now I'm five weeks pregnant with his baby."

-Tiffany Green

Boom! Boom! Boom!
Boom! Boom! Boom!

"I'm coming. I'm coming," Kevin shouted as he hurried downstairs and dashed to his front door.

"Who is that beating on the door like they're crazy?" Rená asked as she rushed down the stairs and looked on while Kevin answered the door.

Kevin peeked out the window. "It's Sistah Green and her husband Ray." He turned and shouted to Rená then opened the door with a welcoming smile. "Hey Brother Ray, Sistah Lin—,"

POP!

"Ooph..." Kevin sounded off. The force of Ray's punch caused him to stagger backward.

POP! Linda reached around her husband and punched Kevin in the face.

Kevin stumbled to the floor, holding his jaw.

Rená quickly ran to her husband's defense. "Stop hitting my husband," she shouted.

Ray pulled out a small handgun from his back pocket and pointed it in Kevin's face.

Rená jumped in front of Ray's gun. "Please, don't shoot my husband," she screamed.

"Get out of the way, First Lady. This ain't got nothing to do with you," Linda yelled at her.

"Please, don't kill my daddy," Kevin's daughter Joann cried from the top of the staircase with her younger brother standing by her side.

Ray looked up at the children crying at the top of the stairs and suddenly came to his senses and quickly put the gun away. "You're not even worth it," he said and spat in Kevin's face.

"What's going on?"Rená cried.

"Your whorish husband got our eighteen-year-old daughter pregnant," Linda shouted.

"What is she talking about?" Rená turned to Kevin.

"I don't know what she's talking about," Kevin lied and shook his head. His mind instantly began recalling the memories of his encounters with Tiffany. His stomach turned. He realized he never used protection. He just assumed she was on birth control. He never thought in a million years she would end up pregnant.

"You ain't gonna stand here in my face and deny my daughter's baby," Linda roared, then lunged at Kevin like a wild woman. Her husband quickly jumped in front of her and held her back.

"MOMMA, STOP!" Tiffany screamed as she stepped through the door. "He doesn't know. I didn't tell him I was pregnant," she cried to her mother. Then she turned and looked Rená in the eyes. "I'm sorry, First Lady, but me and Pastor Tyler have been messin' around for almost two months, and now I'm five weeks pregnant with his baby."

Rená gasped. Tiffany's words hit her like a ton of bricks. Her head began to spin, and she could barely breathe. Her heart beat erratically and she felt as if an elephant stood on her chest. She clutched her heart and dropped to her knees. "Kevin, how could you do this to me?" She whimpered, and then inhaled a deep breath before exhaling an ear-shattering scream.

Linda's anger temporarily disappeared at the sight of her First Lady in pain. She felt sorry for her. She kneeled on her knees and wrapped her arms around Rená's shoulder to comfort her.

For a moment, all eyes were focused on Linda and Rená, when suddenly they heard the loud sound of tires screeching. All their necks instantly snapped around to see what was going on outside in front of the house.

Parnell Snipes swerved his pick-up truck and ran over the curb onto the Tyler's front yard. He jumped out of his vehicle, bolted through the door and began punching Kevin in the face.

"You're the reason Pam left me. You were foolin' around with her all along," Parnell snarled as he repeatedly pounded his fist into Kevin's face.

Parnell's accusations stunned everyone in the house. But none of them bothered to pull him off Kevin, not even Rená. They just stood by and watched as he beat him.

Jackie and Pam were tailing right behind Parnell in Jackie's White Escalade. They were afraid that Parnell would kill Pastor Tyler. After the cancellation of the bus trip, Jackie gave Pam a ride to her new apartment. As they pulled into the apartment complex, they noticed Parnell waiting in front of her door. One of the women from the church bus had called him and told him Pam's confession about sleeping with Pastor Tyler. He intended to beat Pam to death, but Jackie wouldn't let her get out of the SUV. She threatened to call the police on him if he laid a finger on Pam. But when Parnell jumped into his truck, they knew he was heading straight to the pastor's house. Pam quickly dialed 9-1-1 as Jackie sped behind him.

Jackie and Pam rushed through the door of the Tyler's house and saw the horrifying sight of Parnell viciously pounding the bloody face of an unconscious Pastor Tyler.

Tears instantly formed in Jackie's eyes, and she went into a frenzy. "Get off of him," she screamed as she jumped on Parnell's back and clawed away at his eyes.

"Somebody get this crazy woman off of me," Parnell yelled.

Everyone at once rushed to pull Jackie off him, but she clawed and scratched like a madwoman. Finally, Ray managed to wrestle her away as she continued kicking and swinging at Parnell.

The sight of her Pastor lying unconscious in a pool of blood caused Jackie to snap and it was in that moment that she realized what he meant to her.

A police cruiser pulled up in front of the house. After assessing the situation, the police officers arrested Parnell, and Kevin was rushed to the hospital in an ambulance.

****

Chapter 36

"It's too late to be crying and praying now. You should have done all of that before you started having sex with half the congregation."

-Sister Jackie

Kevin awoke dazed and confused. He looked around the strange room and blinked repeatedly. He tried to focus and figure out where he was. After a few seconds had passed, the grogginess began to wear off and he realized he was in a hospital room. He lifted his head slightly off the pillow and noticed Jackie asleep in a chair in the corner of the room. She opened her eyes at the sound of him struggling to sit up in his bed. She smiled and quickly dashed to his bedside.

"Pastor, be careful. Don't try to move too fast."

"What happened? How did I get here?" he asked. The last thing he remembered was being tackled and punched by Pam's husband.

"You were unconscious after Parnell attacked you. The ambulance drove you here. You've been out for nearly two days."

"Where is my wife? Where are Rená and the kids?" he asked as he scanned the room for a sign of his family.

Jackie didn't answer his question. She just looked into his eyes before lowering her head. It wasn't hard for him to read her expression. His wife and kids were gone.

"Did she come to see me while I was out?"

"No...she didn't," Jackie whispered.

"Has she even called to check on me?"

"No." Jackie shook her head.

"What about my children?" His voice quivered.

Jackie raised her head, looked directly in Kevin's eyes, and spoke frankly. "Look, Pastor Tyler. As soon as the ambulance pulled off with you, your wife started packing her things and left with your kids."

Tears rolled down Kevin's face as he thought about the pain and embarrassment he must have caused his family. "Lord, please forgive me for what I have done," he cried as the thought of Tiffany Green carrying his baby ran through his mind. "Jesus, please watch over my family and protect them from any hurt, harm or danger."

"It's too late to be crying and praying now," Jackie snapped at him. "You should have done all of that before you started having sex with half the damn congregation."

Kevin frowned and bucked his eyes at her. "Half the congregation? What are you talking about?" He thought Tiffany and Pam were the only secrets that had been exposed.

"You don't have to play dumb with me. All of your mess is out in the open. You're the talk of the town. Everybody's talking about you and Pam, April, Ms. Barbara Jo, Mary Armstrong, Dottie Ann. I mean, the list of names goes on and on. People are even saying you had something going on with Deron."

"Oh my God..." Kevin groaned and dropped his head back on to the pillow. He couldn't believe his secrets were out for the world to judge him. He wished Parnell had killed him. He didn't know how he was going to face his congregation. He thought about the last words Reverend Stokes said to him. *You'll end up destroying your life and the lives of those people in your congregation.*

"How did my life come to this?" he mumbled to himself, but before he could complete the thought in his head, a nurse entered the room.

"I see you're finally up, Mr. Tyler." The nurse smiled at him. "How do you feel?"

"I'm okay. I just need to get out of here and get home."

"The doctor is gonna have to release you. You suffered some serious injuries," the nurse replied.

"What serious injuries?" Kevin questioned her.

"Mr. Tyler, you have a broken nose, a fractured eye socket, and a concussion."

"I don't care about my injuries. I just need to go home right now."

Jackie noticed he was getting agitated. She reached in her purse, pulled out her compact mirror, and held it in front of his face. Kevin gasped and paused at the gruesome sight looking back at him. Both of his eyes were black, his nose was twisted, and his face was so swollen and deformed that he almost didn't recognize his reflection. He covered his face with his hands and burst into tears.

Tears streamed down Jackie's face as she watched her pastor breakdown. She leaned forward and wrapped her arms around him. "It's going to be alright, Pastor. I've got your back. I'm going to be here to help you get through this."

Jackie held Kevin's hand until the nurse left the room. Once they were alone again, she hit him with more disturbing news. She informed him that the rumors about his affairs had spread around town so quickly since he'd been in the hospital, that the deacon board was planning on meeting to vote him out as pastor. She assured him that she wouldn't allow it to happen without a fight. She explained that as the church's secretary, it was part of her job to know all their bylaws and guidelines. And without evidence, he couldn't be terminated from his position based on hearsay and gossip.

"I don't think any of those women you had sex with will stand in front of the Deacon board and confess to having an affair with you."

"I don't think I deserve to be New Hope's pastor any longer," Kevin said to her.

"Everyone deserves a second chance. Besides, you signed a two-year contract and the church has to honor it or they will have to buy you out."

"I don't need the church's money."

"I know you don't need any money, but you need a second chance."

"No, I don't. I'll sound like a fool calling myself a pastor after all that has been going on in my life."

"Don't worry about that. The preachers around here do it all the time. As long as you look good and can preach good, the people will forgive and forget. Trust me, they will support you again."

Kevin paused for a moment as he thought about what Jackie had just said to him. "Do you think the congregation will still respect me as a pastor after what I've done?

"Pastor Baylor's congregation forgave him. He got caught messin' around with one of the deacon's wives and on top of that, he was having sex with six other women in his church, *and* his wife ended up divorcing him. Now he's married one of the six women he was fooling around with.

Kevin's mouth almost dropped to the floor. "Are you talking about Pastor Baylor over at A New Faith Temple church?"

"Yep, and do you know Reverend Jones over at Mount Zion?" Jackie asked.

"Yeah."

"That's his mistress that's sitting up in the pulpit in the first lady's seat. His wife left him a few years ago after he got caught messin' around with one of his members."

"But I don't want to be known as one of those whorish, skirt-chasing preachers. I wasn't brought up in the ministry like that."

"All I'm saying is that you should keep preaching. We can figure out how to rehabilitate your image."

"What day is the meeting scheduled for?" Kevin asked.

"Don't worry about that. They can't vote you out without you being present to address the allegations, and you can't be present until you have healed from your injuries. So we have a couple of weeks to come up with a plan." She smiled and winked her eye at him as if she already had everything figured out.

Kevin didn't respond; he just stared at her with a blank and confused look on his face.

"What's wrong, Pastor? Why are you looking at me like that?"

"I just wanna know why you're helping me. Why would you stick your neck out for me?"

"Because you're my pastor and I love you. Now get some rest. I'll be here when you wake up." She kissed his forehead, walked back to the chair in the corner of the room, and sat down.

After four days in the hospital, Jackie finally drove Kevin home. Over the next week, she came to his house every evening and checked on him, only staying long enough to drop off his dinner. She didn't want to give people any reason to spread rumors about her. He had already had enough speculation about his extracurricular activities to last him a lifetime.

****

Chapter 37

"Listen to me, preacher, if you ring my doorbell one more time, you're gonna have to whoop me...and I'm a hard old man to whoop..."

-Reverend Carver

After being cooped up in his house for over a week, with no one to talk to, Kevin's mind wandered all over the place. He didn't know what to do. His wife wasn't answering his phone calls, his kids refused to talk to him, and he couldn't call Reverend Stokes after the falling out they had in Atlanta.

The frustration caused unwanted urges to resurface. His body and mind craved the sensual gratifications that only sex could give him. He tried fasting, praying, and reading his Bible, but nothing changed. He even tried reading The Pastor's Book of Warnings, but nothing seemed to ward off the desires burning in his flesh.

He needed someone he trusted to talk with and open up to about his problem. He thought about confiding in Jackie, but he quickly dismissed that idea. The more he saw her, the more he wanted to have sex with her, and he didn't want to ruin their friendship, even though he felt that she wanted to be more than just friends.

Reverend Carver was the only person left he could call. He wanted his opinion on whether he should leave Dyersburg or try to remain the pastor of New Hope. But after calling Reverend Carver's phone for two days without getting an answer, Kevin decided to go to his house to see him in person. He waited to drive over under the cover of night so no one would see him. He was still in hiding. The swelling on his face had gone down, but both of his eyes were still black.

He drove up to Reverend Carver's house and noticed a handful of luxury vehicles parked in the driveway. He recognized two of the cars. The white and gold Cadillac CTS belonged to Bishop Andrews and Pastor Baylor drove the silver Mercedes.

Kevin shook his head. His timing couldn't have been worse. Reverend Carver was having his quarterly get together. Every three months he threw an informal dinner party at his house where he invited a handful of members from the Black Pastor's Association. Kevin and Rená had attended a couple of the gatherings since arriving in Dyersburg.

When he saw all the cars parked outside of Reverend Carver's house, he thought about turning around and going back home. He didn't want to disturb the Reverend's dinner party. Plus, he was too ashamed to face the other preachers. But he wanted to know why Reverend Carver hadn't been answering his calls. Maybe he had changed his number? Despite his feelings of embarrassment, Kevin put on his shades, got out of his car, and press the doorbell.

Mrs. Carver answered the door and jumped when she saw him standing there. She looked as though she'd seen a ghost. Kevin could see in her face that she was surprised at the sight of him.

"Good evening, Pastor Tyler. I wasn't expecting to see you here tonight," she said with a fake smile on her face as she stood, blocking the doorway behind her.

Kevin instantly sensed an awkward vibe coming from her and assumed she had heard the rumors about him "I'm not here for the dinner party. I just need to have a quick word with your husband."

"Wait right here, and I'll go get him for you," she replied before closing the door and leaving him standing outside.

Even though he didn't want to come in, Kevin felt a little disrespected when she didn't invite him into the house. He stood outside for nearly ten minutes before the door opened again.

Reverend Carver came out dressed to kill in a European-fitting Versace suit. He stepped outside and closed the door behind him.

Kevin flashed a huge smile when he saw the Reverend. He felt a sense of relief when he finally saw his friend. "Hey, Reverend, how have you been?" Kevin greeted him with his arms open expecting a warm embrace, but Reverend Carver stopped him. He extended his arm and pushed Kevin back. "What's wrong?" Kevin asked.

Reverend Carver looked around as if he was checking to see if anyone was listening, and then he spoke under his breath to Kevin. "Listen here, Pastor Tyler. I'm gonna have to distance myself from you. You're the talk of the town, and I don't want my ship to sink along with yours."

"But...but..." Kevin tried to explain.

Reverend Carver quickly cut him off. "It was nice knowing you, but I'm gonna have to ask you to leave my house. I wish you well Brother Pastor," he said before quickly returning inside and slamming the door behind him.

Kevin stood there in shock. He couldn't believe Reverend Carver would just blow him off like that. Whom else could he turn to? If anyone could understand what he was going through, it was Reverend Carver. He decided to ring the doorbell again. He wanted to explain himself. He needed his friend to just hear him out.

But this time Reverend Carver answered the door with anger in his eyes. He stepped outside and quickly shut the door behind him. He got in Kevin's face with his fist clenched tight and threatened him.

"Listen to me, preacher. If you ring my doorbell one more time, you're gonna have to whoop me...and I'm a *hard* old man to whoop. Now get away from my house." Reverend Carver lunged forward and pushed Kevin so hard that he stumbled back and fell to the ground.

Kevin sat on the ground and watched Reverend Carver as he walked back into the house. His heart dropped to his stomach. He couldn't remember the last time someone had rejected him like that. Reverend Carver hurt his feelings. Tears welled in his eyes as reality sunk in. He was all alone, no wife, no kids, no Reverend Stokes, and no Reverend Carver.

He slowly got up from the ground and while he dusted himself off, he noticed the other preachers and their wives, staring out of Reverend Carver's giant living room window at him. They quickly looked away when they noticed he saw them.

Kevin walked back to his car and thought about packing up his things and leaving Dyersburg for good. He wanted to go back to Atlanta. He wished he had never taken the job at New Hope. He thought about how good his life was before Dyersburg. "This city is cursed," he said out loud.

He got in his car and looked back at Reverend Carver's house one more time before driving away.

****

Chapter 38

"Maybe this is a sign from God telling me that I need to get myself together."

-Pastor Tyler

A single tear escaped Kevin's eye as he leaned against his kitchen counter and sipped on his coffee. He stared at the papers in his hand and thought about the first time he saw his Renā. He knew she was the one he wanted to spend the rest of his life with. He remembered thanking God after she accepted his marriage proposal. Besides the birth of his children, it was the happiest day of his life.

Just minutes earlier, while fixing his morning cup of coffee, his doorbell rang. He answered the door and there stood a middle-aged white man asking for Kevin Tyler. When he confirmed to the man that he was Kevin Tyler, the man quickly replied to him, "You've been served," and pushed a large yellow envelope into his hand.

The yellow envelope held divorce papers. Renā didn't waste any time. It had barely been two weeks since she'd left. He thought about calling but quickly changed his mind. *What would I even say to her?* he thought.

He shook his head and held back the tears as he thought about his kids. They would have to grow up without their father in the house with them. "Please, God, make this right," he prayed aloud. And while he prayed, his phone vibrated. It was a text from Jackie.

"The meetn wit da Board of Deacons has bn scheduled 4 Thurs. @ 2... Don't 4get our plan. We got this...☺"

When Kevin saw the text, he immediately called her. "Hey, Jackie. I *really* need to see you. Can you come over right now?" he asked. He was ready to throw their friendship out the window. After receiving the divorce papers, sex was the only thing that could ease his mind, and Jackie had been on his radar since he woke up in the hospital.

"I can't. I'm in Nashville at a seminar," she replied. Jackie only worked part-time as the church's secretary. On her real job, she was a probation officer for the Tennessee Department of Corrections, and twice a year, she had to go to Nashville for training.

"Damn!" Kevin blurted out, allowing his frustration to slip-out verbally.

"Pastor, is everything alright?"

"Not really. Rená just had me served with divorce papers, and I just needed a friend right now."

Even though he didn't come right out and say it, she knew exactly what he wanted from her. And now that he had been served with divorce papers, she wouldn't let her conscience get in the way of her feelings for him. "I'll meet you at church Thursday, and we can get together afterward. I gotta go, but I'll call you back later," she said.

Kevin didn't bother to say goodbye to her. He just clicked his phone off and tossed it on to the kitchen table. "Today is Monday. I can't wait until Thursday," he said as he squeezed the coffee cup in his hand. "Damn, Jackie," he shouted as he threw the empty cup against the kitchen wall, causing it to shatter into pieces.

It had been over two weeks since he last had sex, and he felt like he was about to explode. He'd been trying to stay strong and do the right thing, but the divorce papers had pushed him to the edge. "I gotta go get it," he said to himself. And he knew exactly where to go. He quickly freshened up and drove straight to April's house. He didn't even bother to park down the street for discretion. He pulled right in front of her duplex.

However, April refused to let him in. Heartbroken by the revelation of his other affairs. She shouted through the cracked door that she never wanted to see him again and swore she would never step in New Hope Pentecostal Church as long as he was the pastor.

Kevin was angry after talking to April. He couldn't believe that she refused to have sex with him. He never loved her or anything like that, he was even beginning to realize that he didn't even really care about her feelings either. All he wanted was sex. And if she wasn't going to have sex with him, she served no purpose.

His next stop was Pam's apartment, but when he pulled into the apartment complex, he saw Parnell's truck. He didn't want to knock on the door for fear of another beating, so instead, he sat in his car and called to see if she was available.

"Me and Parnell are trying to work things out. He even promised to start going to church with me as long as we don't go to New Hope," she said to Kevin over the phone

He couldn't believe what he heard from Pam's mouth *She was a stupid bitch anyway.* He hung up the phone "If she goes back to him, she's crazier than I thought," he said as he drove off.

One by one, all the women he had been having sex with, turned him down. Carmen, Barbara Jo, Dottie Ann and even Mary Armstrong refused him.

Having nowhere to go and no one to turn to for comfort, Kevin wondered to himself, *Maybe this is a sign from God telling me that I need to get myself together.*

He drove around town for another hour, debating with himself whether he should go home or keep looking for someone to have sex with. Going home to pray for strength and guidance from God was the right choice to make but roaming the streets of Dyersburg for some much-needed sex was an easier choice. It was the choice his flesh wanted, and he reasoned with himself that the only way he would feel better was through sex.

After driving around for hours, Kevin found himself riding down *Crack Alley,* a notorious street on the west side of town, best known for drugs and prostitution.

He quickly spotted two strung-out prostitutes standing on the corner. Looking both frail and haggard, it was obvious the women were in dire need of food and rest. This, however, meant nothing to Kevin whose main concern was to satisfy his sexual needs.

When Kevin's Mercedes stopped at the corner, both women ran to his car.

"Hey, baby, are you looking for a date?" one woman asked as she stuck her head in the open passenger side window.

She was the better looking of the two, but when the woman behind her smiled, he noticed she didn't have any teeth. Kevin's mind began to turn. *I wonder what it would feel like to get oral from a woman without any teeth.* "How much for both of you?" he asked.

"You can get both of us for $100."

"What can I get for $1000?" he asked as he flashed a wad of money in their faces.

"Sweetheart, for $1000 you can get whatever you want and however you want it—from both of us," she replied with an excited smile on her face. Both women then quickly jumped in his car.

****

Chapter 39

"I believed in you; I stuck my neck out for you; I was willing to give my body to you, and oh well is all you have to say."

- Jackie Lawrence

Jackie rushed out of New Hope Church and sped over to Kevin's house. She was worried about him. He hadn't answered any of her calls or returned any of her texts in days. She'd left her weeklong seminar a day early to meet him at church to help him keep his job, and he was a no-show. The Deacons waited over an hour. They were so angry he'd skipped the meeting that they agreed to get rid of him by buying him out of his contract. This was well within their power to do, and there wasn't anything she could do to stop it from happening.

Jackie pressed the doorbell and knocked on the door at Kevin's house for nearly ten minutes. His cars were in the driveway, but no one answered. She tried calling his phone again, but it kept going straight to voice mail.

She turned the doorknob before leaving. It was unlocked. She eased the door open and called out to him. "Pastor Tyler are you in here?" she shouted as she crept through the house.

She noticed that the house was a mess, and she smelled a foul odor. "Pastor Tyler," she continued to yell as she made her way upstairs. And then she heard a faint noise. She paused and tried to follow the sound. It was coming from a closed door. She pressed her ear up against the door before gradually pushing it open.

"PASTOR TYLER!" Jackie shouted as loud as she could. "What the hell are you doing?"

Kevin sat naked on the edge of his bed smoking a crack pipe while watching two of Dyersburg's most well-known prostitutes engaging in lesbian sex.

Jackie's face turned red. She walked over and slapped the crack pipe out of Kevin's hand.

"I've been calling and worrying myself sick about you and you're in here doing drugs and having sex with prostitutes?" At that point, she turned and shouted at the two naked women. "Lulu and Shay, if you two don't put some clothes on and get outta here, I'm gonna violate your probation and have both of your butts put back in jail before nightfall."

Kevin sat on the bed with his mind still fogged from the drugs. "Jackie, what are you doing here? You said you weren't coming back 'til Thursday."

"Today *is* Thursday."

"What time are we supposed to be meeting up at church?" a high and clueless Kevin asked.

"The meeting is over, and they decided to buy you out of your contract."

"Oh well!" Kevin chuckled.

"Oh well, is that all you have to say?" Jackie shouted through tears. "I believed in you; I stuck my neck out for you; I was willing to give my body to you, and oh well is all you can say?" She stared at him.

Kevin was stoned out of his mind, and the only words he heard come out of her mouth was she was willing to give her body to him. He stood up, naked as a bird, with his manhood fully erect, and tried to put his arms around her.

"What are you doing?" she asked.

"Come on, Jackie, baby, you said you wanted to give your body to me."

"Pastor Tyler, stop...please don't...stop it," Jackie screamed as she struggled to wrestle away from him.

But Kevin was horny and high on crack. He didn't realize he was being overly aggressive. He wrapped his arms around Jackie and threw her on the bed. He landed on top of her and pulled her skirt up and positioned himself in between her legs.

"Pastor, stop...please, don't do this... pleeeease," she cried out to him.

But Kevin was like a wild animal being driven purely by his instincts. He couldn't hear her cries. He wanted to have sex with her.

Jackie continued to cry out as he wrestled her down on the bed. She knew he was high and out of his mind, and if he was clearheaded and they were under normal circumstances, she would have given herself to him willingly. She wasn't even struggling with all of her might, because deep down, a part of her wanted him to take her. She had wanted him since they'd first met. But she was not going to allow him to force himself on her after seeing Lulu and Shay in his bed. So, while he was focused on trying to tear her panties off, she reached over, grabbed the lamp off the nightstand beside the bed, and smashed it against his skull.

The sudden blow to the side of his head sobered Kevin up instantly. He rolled off Jackie and onto the floor. Blood spewed out of a large gash in his head. He looked up at Jackie and realized what he almost did to her.

"I'm sorry, Jackie. Please forgive me. I didn't mean to hurt you." He tried to apologize, his hand on his bleeding head. Curling into the fetal position on the floor, he cried and screamed like a baby, while suffering a mental breakdown.

Jackie stood over him and looked down. He was bloody, naked, and curled on the floor. He was no longer the confident, well-dressed man he'd been when they first met. She shook her head. "Look how far you've fallen," she said to him before walking out of the room.

"Jackie, please don't leave me...I need help... please come back...help me, please," Kevin cried out for her as she walked away.

She heard his screaming and wailing as she walked down the stairs and out of the front door. She sat outside of his house in her Escalade and cried. She wanted to go back and help him, but she knew there was nothing else she could do for him. He was beyond her reach. Jackie picked up her phone and called Reverend Stokes. She told him about everything that had happened over the past few months. She gave him the details of the bus confessions, Kevin's stay at the hospital, the Deacon board's decision, and even the attempted rape that had just taken place.

As soon as Reverend Stokes got off the phone with Jackie, he called Deacon Gilbert and within a matter of minutes, they were on their way to Dyersburg.

****

Chapter 40

"You see, I told you God still loves you."

-Reverend Stokes

Jackie had been patiently waiting outside in her Escalade when Reverend Stokes and Deacon Gilbert pulled up at Kevin's house. A few hours earlier, after she first called Reverend Stokes, she went home and took a shower. She had to clean the blood splatter from Kevin's head off her. But she couldn't stay away. She was worried about her pastor, so she drove back to his house and sat outside until help arrived.

Reverend Stokes and Deacon Gilbert got out of the car and quickly followed Jackie into the house. The front door was still unlocked. They followed her upstairs to his bedroom. The door was closed like before, and Jackie didn't know what she would see this time.

"He's in there," she whispered to them as she stepped to the side and pointed at the bedroom door.

Reverend Stokes didn't hesitate. He immediately opened the door with Deacon Gilbert and Jackie following close behind him.

"Kevin, no!" Reverend Stokes screamed.

Jackie heard the fear in Reverend Stokes' voice, but she didn't see Kevin until deacon Gilbert moved to the side. Her heart stopped. She tried to scream but she couldn't force any sound out. She lost her voice at the sight of him sitting on the floor with his back against the wall and a gun in his hand. An empty bottle of wine and a crack-pipe lay on the floor next to him, and he was still naked, with only a bathrobe covering his body. She could see he hadn't bathed since she last saw him six hours ago. The blood from his head wound had dried all over his face and neck.

Kevin looked up when he heard Reverend Stokes voice. He widened his eyes at the sight of the old man.

"Stay away from me," Kevin shouted. He raised the gun and pressed the tip of the barrel to his head. "Stay away or I swear, I'll pull the trigger."

Reverend Stokes stopped in his tracks. He opened his arms wide to block Deacon Gilbert and Jackie from moving forward. "Kevin, what are you doing?" he asked with tears in his eyes. He couldn't believe what he was seeing. He didn't recognize the person in front of him. This wasn't the man he raised in the ministry for over twenty years. "Talk to me, son. Tell me what's going on."

"I'm tired," Kevin cried. "I'm tired of everything. I wanna go be with Big Mike."

Jackie and Deacon Gilbert looked puzzled when he said Big Mike's name. They didn't know who he was talking about.

But Reverend Stokes remembered that day in his office after Big Mike's funeral. The pain of Big Mike's death was what led Kevin to accept Christ in his life.

"Don't do this, Kevin. God still has a purpose for your life." Reverend Stokes tried to speak calmly to him, but he couldn't hide the panic that trembled in his voice. He was scared Kevin would pull the trigger. The broken man on the floor was not just his son in the ministry, he was more like his real son, and he couldn't bear to watch him blow his brains out in front of him.

"I don't want to hear that *God has a purpose for me* mess. God led me to Dyersburg and now look at me. Is this what God wanted?" Kevin continued to cry and vent at the Reverend. "Just Look at me...I ain't got nobody. God done left me all alone... Don't nobody love me... I just wanna go be with Big Mike."

"I love you, son," Reverend Stokes said as tears streamed down his face.

"I love you too," Jackie's voice quivered.

"Me too," Deacon Gilbert added. "Why do you think I drove all the way here? I came because I love you."

Kevin slowly calmed down. Their words touched him. He took a deep breath and lowered his gun. He looked into each of their eyes one by one and realized they were being sincere. They did love him.

Reverend Stokes was relieved when Kevin lowered his gun. "That's right, son. We all love you," he said to Kevin as he eased closer to him. "And most important of all is that God loves you too."

When Kevin heard those words come out of Reverend Stokes' mouth, anger instantly overtook him. He gave Reverend Stokes a look of pure rage, and then he shook his head from side-to-side. "You're wrong, Reverend. God doesn't love me." He suddenly raised the gun back up to his head and quickly pulled the trigger.

"Nooo..." Reverend Stokes shouted.

Jackie instinctively closed her eyes and turned her head.

Click...The gun didn't fire.

Click...Click...Kevin pulled the trigger two more times, and nothing happened.

Reverend Stokes lunged at Kevin and grabbed his hand. Kevin dropped the gun, fell into Reverend Stokes' arms, and cried like a baby.

"I've got you, son," his beloved mentor whispered in his ear.

Jackie kneeled on the floor, putting her arms around them while praising and thanking God.

Deacon Gilbert picked the gun up from the floor and said aloud, "Thank God this gun jammed. The firing pin must be damaged." He examined the gun for a few seconds and then he extended his arm straight up, pointing the gun to the ceiling, and pulled the trigger.

POW...The gun fired. The loud sound caused everyone to jump.

Kevin raised his head from Reverend Stokes' shoulder. He looked up at the hole in the ceiling and at that moment, he looked up at Reverend Stokes.

"You see, son, I told you. God Still loves you," Reverend Stokes said.

THE END

Epilogue

"You were only here for ninety days, now you have the rest of your life ahead of you. Take it one day at a time and one battle at a time," the therapist Ms. Carla said to Kevin and then she leaned in and gave him a supportive back patting hug.

"Thank you. This place has really made a difference in my life."

"Are you sure you don't wanna come back as an in-house counselor? With your pastoral experience, you could really help a lot of people."

"I appreciate the offer but right now I just wanna get back to my family," Kevin said. "I think that's them there." He smiled as he jutted his chin towards the glass double doors at the car pulling up in front of the building.

The car stopped and Jackie appeared out of the rear door. Other than Reverend Stokes, she was the only person he had been in contact with since admitting himself into the clinic.

For the first thirty days during his electronics restrictions, they wrote letters to each other. The next thirty days they emailed back and forth, and they video chatted daily for the final thirty days of his stay.

Her eyes lit up when she first saw Kevin, then they exploded with tears of joy. She ran and jumped into his arms, wrapping her legs around his waist, with her arms gripped tightly around his neck. She nearly knocked him down.

"I love you so much," she whimpered in his ear. Her tears soaked the side of his face.

After a long suffocating kiss, she released him and smiled while wiggling her fingers in front of his face. "How does it look in person."

"It's beautiful." Kevin grinned. "But I'm gonna get you another one when I propose to you the right way."

"What does that mean?"

"You deserve more than a FaceTime proposal and I couldn't find the ring I really wanted online."

"Well, it's perfect to me. I love my five carats." She held her hand up admiring her ring. "And we already have a wedding date, so there's no reason to propose again. Our engagement is official."

"Where's Reverend Stokes?" Kevin asked as he looked around and tried to focus to see if there was anyone else in the backseat of the Uber. "I thought y'all were flying out together."

Jackie lowered her head and then grabbed both of Kevin's hands. "I'm sorry sweetheart but she told me not to tell you over the phone."

"Who is she. And tell me what!" Kevin's voice shrieked as he stepped back pulling his hand free.

"Mrs. Stokes," Jackie blurted out. "Reverend Stokes had a heart attack three days ago."

"Is he dead?" Kevin's voice tremored.

"Initially he was in a coma, but I got the call this morning before I boarded my flight that he had passed overnight."

Kevin's eyes widened and his mouth hung open as he stared back into Jackie's face. He couldn't process what she had just said to him. He was speechless. His chest tightened and heat flashed from the back of his ears down his neck. Then suddenly, her words caught up to his emotions and he belted out a loud wail and dropped to his knees, with his hands covering his face.

Jackie moved in closer, allowing him to bury his head into her midsection, muffling his crying. "I got you sweetheart," she whispered as she caressed his head.

***

"That was a powerful message you delivered. I see why the family wanted you to preach Brother Stokes' homegoing," Bishop Mathews leaned over and said to Kevin as they sat beside each other.

"Thank you," Kevin responded dryly.

"This is also a nice repast, the food is delicious," he said to Kevin.

"Yes, it is, Deacon Gilbert and Sistah Angela did an amazing job." Kevin replied.

A strange silence loomed in the air as they ate. Kevin wasn't in much of a mood for conversation. He had just buried his mentor, and this was his first time seeing Rena since she left him in Dyersburg. It had been awkward walking in with Jackie while Rena was there.

"I know this isn't the best time but since I'm here in person, I'd like to run something by you," Bishop Mathews said.

"What's on your mind?"

"Do you want the vacant pastor's position here?"

"You've got to be kidding," Kevin shot back at him.

"No, I'm serious."

"Why would the bishop board want to give me the job?"

"We didn't vote to give it to you. The Reverend's grandfather founded this church, and they later joined our denomination. They were allowed to keep one clause in their bylaws."

"What does that have to do with me?"

Bishop Mathews looked around and then lowered his voice. "The clause is that the outgoing Pastor is allowed to name his successor."

"There has to be a mistake. Reverend Stokes wouldn't do that after everything I've been through."

"Well he did, and he had the opportunity to change it, but he didn't. So the job is yours if you want it."

"How do you feel about it?" Kevin asked.

"I believe everyone deserves a second chance."

Kevin sat and thought about it for a few minutes. And then he turned to Bishop Mathews and said, "Let me talk it over with Jackie and I'll give you an answer in a couple of days."

****

Words From the Author

The Preacher's Addiction was an absolute joy for me to write. I typed the first draft more than four years ago. And since then, I have passed the manuscript to friends and family, and they all loved the story. However, each of them had their own opinion they wanted to express to me about certain characters and the different subject matter within the book. This would lead to hours of conversations. *Their opinions versus my opinions, and They would have done this as opposed to why a character did that.*

I thoroughly enjoyed all the dialogue the story sparked. Some of my early readers would call me up and say, *I asked my sister or mother about this or that.* This would lead to even more opinions and conversations, and I loved it. I learned so much about my friends and family.

The ten questions in the back of the book were some of the main topics of our discussions. I added them there for you, to share your opinions with one another or to simply spark dialogue.

I decided to design two covers for this book after going back and forth with my editor. I submitted the manuscript to her under the genre of Urban fiction. But less than seventy-five pages into the first round of editing, she asked if I was going for urban fiction or Christian fiction. I remembered having the same conversation with my brother Keith.

The Preacher's Addiction is urban fiction. It just happens to be about Christian characters dealing with genuine issues.

Since the questions are Christian based, I created the alternate cover with a clean version for my Christian/Church audience. Once you read the story, you're gonna want to discuss the issues with someone you know.

Thank you,

R. T. Haymon

Now that you've finished reading this book, it would mean the world to me if you would scan the QR code below and leave your honest opinion and review on Amazon.

Scan to follow on Facebook

Questions for Group discussion

1) Do you believe sexual addiction is a real diagnosis like alcohol and drug addiction?

2) Is it okay for a Christian to watch pornography in the privacy of his or her own home?

3) Do you believe oral sex is permissible in a Christian marriage? (Why or why not) Explain your answer.

4) Should Kevin ever be allowed to pastor another church? (Why or why not) Explain your answer.

5) Whom should a wife have more respect or reverence for, her husband or her pastor? (Explain your answer.)

6) How would you handle the situation, if you found out your married pastor was having an affair with another member of your church?

7) Can a Christian marriage survive infidelity? If so, how many times should a husband or wife forgive their spouse for cheating? (Explain your answer)

8) Did Pam make the right decision by staying in her marriage and trying to work things out with her husband?

9)Is it okay for a Christian woman to divorce her husband for being physically abusive?

10) Did Kevin take advantage of the women in his church, or do they share in the blame?

www.ingramcontent.com/pod-product-compliance
Lightning Source LLC
Chambersburg PA
CBHW070100260626
47160CB00004B/1264